PROMETHEUS ASCENDS

PROMETHEUS ASCENDS

THE GREAT INSURRECTION™ BOOK SIX

DAVID BEERS

MICHAEL ANDERLE

DISRUPTIVE IMAGINATION

THE PROMETHEUS ASCENDS TEAM

Thanks to our Beta Readers

Kelly O'Donnell, John Ashmore

Thanks to our JIT Readers

Dave Hicks
Peter Manis
Dorothy Lloyd
Diane L. Smith
Jeff Goode
Rachel Beckford
Jackey Hankard-Brodie
Angel LaVey

Editor

SkyHunter Editing Team

DEDICATION

For my brother, Danny.

— David

*To Family, Friends and
Those Who Love
to Read.
May We All Enjoy Grace
to Live the Life We Are
Called.*

— Michael

THE WRITTEN HISTORY OF THE GREAT INSURRECTION

Prometheus' legend continued to grow. It was perhaps the greatest blessing and greatest curse.

Warlords wouldn't come after us anymore; they'd learned that their powers could never match his. No matter how large their army or how advanced their tech was, they'd fail.

A faint line was starting to show up, though, and one thing about Prometheus was he didn't need to be taught a lesson twice. He wouldn't take his eyes away from our goal ever again; nothing would distract him from getting back to Earth and overthrowing the Commonwealth. His obsession returned, but this time, nothing could pull him away from it.

He was the first one to understand the line, and he was the one who told us it would darken—the starkness of one side compared to the other.

The Commonwealth against us.

Prometheus' victories spread across ships, planets,

space stations, and galaxies. His reason spread, too. It couldn't have been helped, even if we'd wanted to.

People had to pick a side as we started back. Planets we came across or dreadnoughts we passed in the darkness of space—for better or worse, we were a target.

A target to hitch your ship to.

Or a target to hit with your weapons.

The closer we moved to the stargate that would take us to the Milky Way, the larger that target grew.

Prometheus saw it before we did, and soon, we couldn't help but see it too. We had grown too large and too strong to move unnoticed. The Commonwealth's spies no longer needed to work the back channels to find out what he was doing.

The line was being drawn. You were for us or against us.

The only thing we couldn't track was the AllSeer's movements. We'd neither heard nor seen anything from him, not since Prometheus had laid his general low. If he was chasing us, he was too far away for even Pro to see it.

Prometheus showed us the line, with us on one side and the Commonwealth on the other. What none of us saw, including him, was the noose being tightened around his neck.

CHAPTER ONE

Caius de Gracilis thought the Imperial Ascendant's last move had been masterful. With a single sentence, he'd upset a game that had been moving against him without his knowing it.

Alexander de Finita had called Caius to the throne room, then he'd asked him a simple question.

"Would you support the marriage of your grandson and Kane's wife?"

Caius was careful to show nothing on his face but said, "I don't mean to question your wisdom, my liege, but would that be a wise choice? Would it not...anger the Titan even more?"

"*Former* Titan, Caius," the Ascendant said from his throne.

"Of course, my liege. Former Titan. Would it anger him more? Is provoking him something we should do?"

"I don't think of it as provoking him, Caius. I think of it as ripping his heart out. How many trillions of kilometers away is he now? By all accounts, he's moving toward the stargate and will be coming back to our galaxy."

Caius looked at his feet for a second, trying to make a decision about something he hadn't seen coming.

"Is there some other reason you don't like the planned marriage?" the Ascendant asked.

Caius shook his head and raised his eyes to Alexander's. "No. You might be right. It might weaken Kane, and I give my full support to anything that will do that."

A masterful stroke. Caius was still impressed two days later.

He and Hector had gone a few thousand kilometers from the Imperial Residence. Caius wanted to spend a few hours out there before heading back. They were hiking through red mountains and canyons, rocks that had been there for millions of years and would be for millions more.

Caius' normal long robe had been shortened and the sleeves removed so he could walk in the tremendous heat without keeling over. He had the StealthBlanket in his robe's pocket. The Ascendant would know they'd made this trip—at such a crucial time—and though they were far away, Caius was prepared for the potential of Alexander listening in.

They'd mostly been silent on their ride here, discussing little more than the weather. Of course, Caius understood that Ascendant understood *why* he'd taken this trip, but it was necessary.

Because Hector wouldn't be leaving Earth any time soon.

Now, with the transport two kilometers behind them,

grandfather and grandson walked over the ancient rocks, taking in the views all around them.

"He's pushing you into a realm you're not prepared for, Hector." The older man went to the cliff's edge and looked down at the long fall beneath him. "It's one your father would have been able to maneuver even better than me, just as you're a finer warrior than me, but to put you here? It shows the Ascendant is more clever than I gave him credit for, and that's my fault." He was mostly talking to himself, but he looked over his shoulder at the hulking mutant behind him. "You'll be staying on Earth while I go back to Mars to prepare for war."

"Why wouldn't the bride and I go back?" Hector asked.

Caius smiled somewhat sadly. He'd planned for so long, and he'd thought this war would be the time his family would take charge. However, now the warrior had to become the politico, and there wasn't enough time to train him. "Luna Kane will never be let out of the Ascendant's custody. She is his trump card since as long as he holds her, the husband *must* take that into account."

The old man turned to look at the old rock. It would outlast them all, remaining until the sun exploded. In some ways, he saw it as a metaphor for the Commonwealth. The government—the bedrock on which society was built—had outlasted generations of men. Was this Titan the supernova that would destroy it?

"I understand," his grandson said after a few moments.

Of course he understood. He wasn't an imbecile, just untrained in such matters.

"The Ascendant is right, though...or he could be. This

might enrage the Titan, or it might break his heart. If it enrages him, our plan is still in play. You'll be needed on the battlefield worse than ever."

"If it breaks him?"

Caius shrugged. "Then our family doesn't deserve to rule, Hector, since the Ascendant was smarter. For all our games, it's the Commonwealth that truly matters—who is the most fit to rule it. If he's more fit than we are, so be it." He paused for a second. "You've met the lady, yes?"

"Yes," the giant responded.

"What do you think of her?"

Hector was quiet for some time. Caius was patient with his grandson; it wasn't his fault he couldn't comment on things of this nature immediately. Caius didn't know if he'd ever had a woman in his bed, let alone be able to navigate this coming marriage.

Hector walked to the very edge of the cliff, then agilely took a seat. His legs dangled.

"She'll never love me. I think she may hate me because she sees me as an extension of the Ascendant. She'll never bend the knee, not when weapons are drawn."

Caius was staring at his grandson, shocked to hear such words coming from him.

Hector didn't look up. "She knows the political games. She may even be a genius with them. Everything she does is perfect, and no one can fault her for a single word. I've seen men like her, though. Men who are entirely committed to their revolutionary leader, but when captured, they will act like they're your servant. When the leader rushes to the door because the enemy has come, that servant will stab you in the back. That's who this woman is."

"How do you know?" Caius asked.

Hector picked up a pebble at his side and tossed it up. His left hand snatched it out of the air like a viper, then, in a fluid motion, launched it off the cliff. "It's in her eyes. If the Ascendant doesn't see it, then he's a fool. She'll kill me the moment she gets a chance, and if I try to bed her, she might kill me before she can try to do it in secret. The woman loves that Titan, and whatever reasons she has to be here, they eventually will serve him."

Caius looked up, his eyes wide. It was rare that Caius misjudged something this late in life, but he'd done it twice recently—once with the Ascendant and now with his grandson's perceptions. "Have you told any of this to Alexander?"

Hector's head whipped upward, confusion on his face. "To the Imperial Ascendant? Of course not. I've told no one but you."

Caius chuckled, then bent and patted his grandson's shoulder. "You're a good man. Marry her and keep that knowledge in your own head for now. Let me think about it some. Remember, our primary goal is to shepherd the Commonwealth past this threat, but the secondary goal is to see who is stronger, de Finita or us."

"Should I bed her?"

The old man frowned in thought. "Will she do it willingly?"

"I don't think so. She loves her husband, and she'd die before that."

Caius shook his head. "We're not rapists. If she won't go to bed with you, then you do your best to shield that from the Ascendant. If he does find out, we'll deal with it then. The Commonwealth may have dishonorable aspects, but we won't win it by losing ourselves to dishonor."

Grandfather and grandson stared into the valley before them, the sun dying behind them.

The wedding was a week away.

The wedding had been a beautiful affair so far, and now the nuptials would take place.

Alexander de Finita, second of his name, Imperial Ascendant of the Commonwealth, sat behind the bride and groom while the guests were in front. His throne put him a half-meter above them as he presided over the most holy of unions.

His robe was deep purple, the only color other than white for the entire wedding. The flowers that decorated the courtyard had been replanted for this occasion, all the purple color of his robe. Only white and purple were allowed, including the clothing of the guests.

Alexander had planned this down to the exact details, including what he would say next.

He'd reverted to extremely old doctrine that allowed the woman's father to give her away. Even that had a reason, though. Luna's father? He was just glad to be able to see his daughter again, and Alexander had sat down with the man for a few hours.

In the end, the father wasn't much different from anyone else vying for power. Of course, he had no idea about Kane still being alive or Luna knowing it. He and the bride would keep that from her father.

The questions came next, and Alexander stood. He didn't step down from the throne, remaining above everyone in the small ceremony.

"Do you take this woman to be your wife?"

"I do," the killer giant said.

"And you, Luna, do you take this man to be your husband?"

"I do." Her voice was little more than a whisper, and her face showed no emotion.

"As the Imperial Ascendant of the Commonwealth, which endows me with all the privileges and responsibilities of said title, I pronounce you husband and wife. May love guide you through the rest of your lives." He looked directly forward, staring into a camera that only a select few knew was filming. "You may kiss your bride, Hector."

<hr>

Luna remembered her first wedding.

Or rather, she remembered *blurs* from her first wedding. Everything had come and gone so fast. There were so many people to see, so many people to thank, that it made it impossible to remember everything. Not to mention that alcohol had flowed freely. Her father had been more than happy to pay for it all, and Luna had been more than happy to partake.

It'd been one of the happiest evenings of her life. Allie in his Titan's uniform, looking beyond handsome.

For this second wedding, Luna remembered *everything*. She didn't partake of any alcohol, and there was no one to see. No one to thank. She knew she was doing an awful job of keeping up appearances, but she was hardly able to make herself smile.

The kiss, when the giant man named Hector had taken her in his arms, had been dead. There was no emotion, no lust… Nothing.

As the reception was winding down, the guests getting ready to depart, Luna slid a steak knife into her dress's long sleeves. She had made it as far as she could, but she was at her wits' end. She knew she couldn't sleep with another man and meet Allie again, look him in the eye.

He would forgive her, of course, given the circumstances.

She wouldn't forgive herself, however. She'd rather die than enter another's bed, and that was what she planned on doing tonight.

Luna knew she couldn't kill this monster. He dwarfed Alistair. He dwarfed *any* man that she'd ever seen, even any mutant. He was big in the way that galaxies were big. Luna could no more kill him than she could throw the moon into the sun. However, the knife now in her sleeve wouldn't be used to cut bread. She would try her best to murder him the moment he placed a hand on her, and then she would die.

Luna kept her face stiff throughout the wedding, even at the end, when her parents came to hug and kiss her goodnight. They would be staying the evening in the Imperial Residence. They'd been quite impressed with the Ascendant's presentation.

Her father had asked her only once if this was too fast.

Luna knew the Ascendant was listening, so with her back toward her father, she told him she loved this new man.

As they prepared to make their way to the matrimonial suite, Luna hugged her mother and kissed her cheek. Her father took her in his arms next and she squeezed him tight, having to close her eyes to keep the tears from flowing down her face.

"I love you, Dad."

He pulled back, likely hearing the pain in her voice. His arms circled her shoulders lightly. "You okay, dear?"

Her lips were tight, and she couldn't speak. All she could do was nod. She'd come too far to break down now. She'd wait until the man tried to take her, then all the rage and pain she'd felt over the past months could come out in one smooth arc when her hand rose toward the monster's neck.

"Okay, dear. I'll see you in the morning," her father said with a measured look.

Another nod.

A few more goodbyes, then the newlyweds were left on their own.

Neither said anything as they made their way to their new suite. Luna kept her eyes on the floor. She knew much about her true husband's legendary physiology. His heartbeat never rose above a certain level, his blood pressure the same. It didn't matter what situation he was put in.

As the elevator rose to their room, Luna wished she had

the same ability. Her heart felt like it might break through her chest wall. She could hear it in her ears and feel it in her temples. Luna saw the man's massive legs next to her petite ones and understood there was nothing she could do to him. Nothing.

The elevator's doors slid aside, and the monster let her off first. It opened directly into their suite, and while the views and architecture might be wonderful to look at, Luna saw none of it.

Luna stepped out and stopped, her head turning to the bedroom on her left.

What do I do, Allie? Do I kill him here, or do I wait until he's in bed? What's going to give me the best result?

Wait, Allie told her, his voice sure and solid. *Wait until he's excited, love, then do it.*

Luna understood what her version of Alistair was saying, but she didn't know if she could kill Hector. She couldn't even pretend to like the monster.

Her new husband stepped around her and pulled a black orb from inside his jacket. He placed it on an end table, then pressed a button on top.

He didn't look at her as he spoke. His back was to her, his head angled so he watched the orb his hand still rested on. "This will keep our conversations and movements private, though it can't be kept on all the time, or those watching will grow suspicious. I imagine you plan on using the knife to kill me if I try touching you. I have no plans to do that, so you can discard the blade. If you wish to try to kill me no matter what, I'll be forced to eliminate you, Luna Kane."

She was stunned. Her left hand went to her right wrist, feeling for the hidden weapon.

The giant continued, "If we're to keep this ruse up, certain things must be...*pretended*. Tonight, I'll have to lie on top of you, and certain...motions and sounds will have to be made. There's no way around that, I'm afraid, because as I'm sure you're aware, eyes are watching. I give you my word that I mean you no harm and seek to have no intimate knowledge of you. We have to act these things out, at least for a time, but we can do it in ways that leave us both clothed."

He paused, placing his hands behind his back.

"If you refuse to go along with these fictions, then keep the blade and attempt to kill me. One way or another, this marriage goes forward or ends tonight. I'm going to leave that choice up to you."

Luna remained motionless for a few seconds. She didn't know how to respond, although she appreciated what he was saying. The monster understood *that* part of her—she'd rather die than sleep with him, and he was okay with it. Yet, he'd keep the charade going.

It all came down to one thing. Luna couldn't kill this man, and the only way to move ahead was by doing as he said: continue the charade.

She let the blade slide out of her sleeve. She stepped next to the monster, careful not to touch him, and laid the knife on the table next to the orb.

Luna gave him a wide berth and went to the bedroom. She left the door open, knowing that closing it would be pointless.

Tears dropped down her face, though. She couldn't

hold them back. She didn't know how that orb out there worked, but she hoped the monster was smart enough to keep it on as she collapsed to the floor and sobbed.

Luna's own shaking hands were the only solace she found.

Please, Alistair. Please. Come home. Come to me.

CHAPTER TWO

Thoreaux hadn't looked to see when the holovid was originally recorded. It was sometime in the past, though obviously not *too* distant.

He was no longer looking at the holovid. He knew what was on it. The entire council did; it'd only taken a few minutes for everyone to understand this was a cruel, *cruel* message.

Luna Kane, in all her beauty, stood in front of the biggest man Thoreaux had ever seen. Perhaps he was as big of some of the gigantes, though at that size, what did it even matter?

Thoreaux's attention had turned to Prometheus, his leader.

For it was his wife on the holovid, wearing a virgin's white and about to marry another man.

Thoreaux had seen the person officiating at the ceremony dressed in royal purple just behind the new bride and groom. The Imperial Ascendant.

Prometheus' eyes were narrowed, and for the first time

Thoreaux could remember, a vein was throbbing on his temple. A table stood just behind Pro, and he stepped to it. His hands found the edge, and it creaked as he gripped its edge. His knuckles were white.

Only three others were in the room: Relm, Servia, and Faitrin.

Thoreaux saw that they were all staring at Prometheus too, none concerned any longer with what the holovid said.

"Leave me," Prometheus commanded.

Relm opened his mouth to say something, and thank the gods, Thoreaux caught his attention. He gave a sharp shake of his head, and Relm's mouth audibly snapped shut.

Everyone but Thoreaux left the room with their heads down.

"Leave me," Pro repeated without looking at him. He stared at the holovid, the wedding still going.

"I'm going to," Thoreaux responded. He didn't step closer to his leader. He doubted Prometheus would harm him or any other of his council, but... Well, he'd never seen a vein pulsing on his leader's forehead either. "I just want you to remember that this is all a game to people like that. He's moving his pieces over the board, and that's all it is— just a move. You know your wife, and you know the only other option the Ascendant would give her was death. Ask yourself if you'd rather have her remarried and alive or married to you and dead?"

"Go," was his only response.

Thoreaux nodded and headed out of the small room. He turned into the hall as the door closed behind him. The other three were waiting for him a couple of meters away.

"What's this mean?" Servia asked as he approached.

Thoreaux shrugged as he walked past the group. "How do I know? He kicked me out just like the rest of you. All I know for certain is that the Ascendant just made this personal in a way he might not understand."

"Did you see the fuckin' vein pop out on his forehead?" Relm asked from the rear. "I thought he might pull his Whip right there and cut the whole ship to pieces. We'd just be icicles floating out in space when he got finished."

"We saw it, Relm," Faitrin assured him.

"Look," Thoreaux said as they turned a corner, "there's a lot to be done, and Pro knows that. He's gonna need some time to deal with what just happened, but it's not our business. *Our* business is getting us back to the Milky Way. I for one don't want him coming out of the room and asking us questions we can't answer."

"True enough," Servia said from just behind him.

The crew split up, and Thoreaux continued walking but made a slight detour before his final stop on the bridge. He'd learned a lot from Pro since meeting him on Pluto. Thoreaux was closer to him than anyone besides perhaps Obs, and he understood that the torture inside the man was much more than he ever showed his subordinates. The only time *they* saw it was when he needed their advice. When he couldn't figure a way out of the situation.

Thoreaux learned that he couldn't show his own torment to those looking to him for answers either. He could only reveal those emotions upward, and right now wasn't one of those times. Truthfully, he didn't have a fucking clue what to think about the wedding and how it'd affected Pro. He couldn't even imagine what the man was thinking, and if he tried to imagine a similar situation regarding Faitrin, revulsion and rage welled up inside him.

All he could do was hope Prometheus had learned his lesson about taking his focus away from their goal.

Thoreaux finally reached the garden area. Since leaving the gigantes' homeworld, Prometheus had put Thoreaux in charge of making sure that those involved in their insurrection could survive long-term without the need for a planet. Pro himself wasn't good at those types of tasks, only conceiving of them. Thoreaux understood that sustainability meant a food source, and that meant gardens. It would be a slow process to get them up and running across the fleet's dreadnoughts, as well as being able to sustain such a large army as they now had. However, Prometheus was right: sustainability took precedence over almost anything else.

The AllMother spent a lot of time in the garden. She hardly ever attended council meetings. Her recovery wasn't complete yet, and if regaining her abilities was required for her to be "complete," Thoreaux thought her recovery wouldn't ever reach that level.

Defending that building had changed the AllMother, and Thoreaux couldn't help but wonder if it had been worth it. If they wouldn't need her in the future, and they hadn't burned her out far too soon.

Were the people she'd saved worth the sacrifice she'd made?

He'd never asked her that question, but as he stepped into the garden, he wondered about it once again. He wondered if losing her mental abilities would affect her ability to continue living. If they had somehow helped keep her alive, what would it mean now that they were gone?

Bright light shone down from above. Walls of fans lined the room, helping to ensure that the correct levels of oxygen versus carbon dioxide remained constant. Green plants sat in rows a bit lower than Thoreaux's waist; the watering system ran up from the floor. He had considered using different methods, including letting the water rain from the ceiling, but the least wasteful method fed the roots and dirt surrounding them without any loss of the precious moisture.

The AllMother sat in a simple fold-out chair the gigantes had built back on their planet. She usually asked someone to carry it for her since the thing was made out of heavy wood. She often sat at one end of the garden and alternated between watching the plants and gardeners or reading.

Her DataTrack was on her lap now, though she wasn't reading. Her eyes were staring at some ripening tomatoes on her left.

She looked up at the sound of Thoreaux's footsteps. Before that last battle, the old woman would have known he was coming at nearly the same time he did.

"Thoreaux, what gives me the pleasure of seeing you today?"

"Just wanted to check on you," he said as he reached her chair. "What are you reading?"

She looked down at the DataTrack. "Novels from before my time. Say what you will about all the great things the Commonwealth gave humanity, art surely wasn't improved."

"How're you feeling, Mother?"

She shrugged, and her gaze fell on the tomatoes again. "I'm doing okay, but I'm tired a lot. Sitting in here helps. I don't know if it's the oxygen or the plants or the lights from above, but I don't feel nearly as sleepy in here." She was quiet for a second, then without looking at him, asked, "How's our leader?"

She would likely have felt something from him; she was asking out of curiosity.

"Right now?" Thoreaux said. "Probably not too well. The Ascendant just pulled a pretty dirty trick."

Still, the AllMother didn't look at him. "He hasn't asked for me, has he?"

"No, ma'am."

She nodded. "Good. You let him know I'm here if he needs me. I don't know how much help I can be now, though."

Thoreaux placed his hand on her shoulder. The old woman looked up and smiled at him. "Thank you for coming by, Thoreaux. You're doing an excellent job with this garden. I can hardly believe there are more like it across so many ships."

"I'm trying." He glanced at the different vegetables. He understood why she liked this place. He liked it too, though he couldn't spend much time here. "I've got to head to the bridge. I just wanted to stop by and say hey. We should do dinner this week. I know Faitrin would like it."

She patted the hand on her shoulder. "Sure, Thoreaux. Sure. Just let me know when."

He gave her shoulder a light squeeze and then turned toward the exit. He knew there would be things on the bridge he had to address, so as he left, he let his worries about the AllMother fade.

The AllMother watched Thoreaux go. The door to the garden opened, then closed, and she was alone once again.

For many years, the AllMother had thought she was alone atop the mountain she'd created, unable to truly be emotionally or intellectually intimate with anyone. Everyone had wanted her attention then, but she'd only been able to share part of herself with a few of her people.

Now, very few people wanted her attention, and she wasn't sure what she could share with any of them. She wasn't sure what she could offer.

The AllMother understood what she'd done to herself, and she thought everyone else did too.

Caesar and Relm were alive because of it, even if a part of her had died.

The AllMother sighed and looked down at the Data-Track. She'd recently found a writer named Stephen King, who'd lived about a hundred years before her birth. He'd written some ghastly stuff, but the AllMother found it hard to pull away and read someone else. Just about the only other thing she liked doing nowadays was watching the plants grow.

For some reason, she liked to see life begin.

Maybe because hers was at an end.

Is it, old woman? something in her asked. It sounded an awful lot like her brother when they were younger. When their names had been different.

She didn't know where her brother was, or what he was doing. She wondered if he knew she'd lost her abilities and whether that changed his plans. Was it still their fate to be together again, or had she lost what he wanted?

As she looked at the red tomatoes, a chill ran down her back.

She knew the truth—the answer to that question.

Nothing would ever stop him. If she died, he'd come for her bones. The AllSeer would carry them around in a bag, a macabre assurance that he would never lose her again.

The AllMother was quiet much of the time now, and she didn't offer anyone her thoughts or training. When she wasn't reading or watching plants grow, she thought about her brother. He was still out there, and she understood that Alistair's mind was more focused on the Commonwealth, which was where it should be.

The rest of her children might think her time as an active force in the movement was nearly done, and for the most part, perhaps that was true. Even so, it was her job to remember her brother since he was surely remembering them.

There wasn't anything she could do at the moment, but it was enough to know that Alexander de Finita, first of his name, was still out there—and his hunt continued.

Alistair watched his wife kiss another man and thought he might vomit. His stomach churned, and he felt acid rise into his throat. it might have been the first time his body had physically reacted to outside stimuli.

The room was now empty, and the holovid was coming to an end. Alistair looked on, unable to pull his eyes away. It wasn't his wife that he focused on, but the man behind the newly wedded couple.

The Imperial Ascendant, Alexander de Finita, second of his name.

Alistair didn't need anyone to tell him this was a ploy. He understood the game the Ascendant was playing. He wanted the rage Alistair now felt to blind him. The Ascendant wanted Alistair to make a mistake, leaving himself open to be killed.

It was more than that, though.

He was letting Alistair know how much he controlled. No matter what Alistair did, de Finita sat back on Earth with Alistair's wife under his thumb.

Obs lay across the room, the only being still in the room with him. His head was between his paws, and his eyes focused on Alistair. He could see the frozen holovid where it hung, but he'd watched enough of it.

Alistair's jaw muscles flexed as he gritted his teeth.

He couldn't do anything from here. Staring at the man would no more hurt him than praying to the gods for his demise. Alistair couldn't think about what would happen to Luna after this ceremony. He couldn't consider what it would be like when he finally saw her. He had to trust that his wife was making the only decisions she could to keep herself alive.

She wasn't betraying him.

Never, Allie, her voice whispered inside his head. *I'm yours, always and forever, in this life and the next.*

Alistair had to get back to her. Everything else...it was

all superfluous. He had to get back to Luna, and he had to end this. The things he'd been through? They were nothing, compared to the horrors she was being forced to endure.

His eyes flashed to Obs, and for the first time, he realized there were tears in them. The room was blurry. His drathe was blurry.

"I'm failing her," he whispered to the animal.

Obs stood up and padded to the other side of the room.

Alistair released the table and sat down. The drathe curled up between his legs.

"I'm failing her," he repeated, and buried his head in the drathe's fur. His hands dug deep into the animal's pelt, but Obs didn't pull away. He let his master tug on him and cry. "I'm failing her."

Long minutes passed as Alistair held his companion and thought about his wife. The holovid remained active, frozen on the Ascendant's eyes and the smirk on his face.

Alistair knew he couldn't stay on the deck crying like this forever, but it was Obs who straightened him up. He let his master hold him for a while but finally forced himself up on all fours and pushed Alistair over.

The former Titan lay on his back, eyes red, face wet, staring up at the drathe.

Obs leaned over and licked Alistair's face with his rough tongue.

Alistair still didn't move, not even to wipe the saliva off his cheeks.

The drathe placed one foot on his master's chest and lowered his snout to just above Alistair's face, then showed his teeth and gave a low growl.

The message was pretty simple. Obs was going to kick Alistair's ass if he didn't get up and get back to work.

Alistair chuckled, finally using his palm to clean his face. "Get off me, ya dumb dog."

The growl grew louder for a moment, but Obs bounded off. Alistair sat up and wiped his face once more, then climbed to his feet and glanced at the holovid. There were no tears in his eyes now.

Obs looked at his master with narrowed eyes as if trying to figure out what the next moment would bring.

Alistair nodded at the holovid.

"I'll be there soon, you son-of-a-bitch. We'll see if you're smiling then."

CHAPTER THREE

The three tentacled creatures slowed.

The closest equivalent to what they felt was "taste." They could taste their target's DNA; it was in the third dimension and very close to where they were in the fifth.

They knew the target wasn't there; the DNA was older and slowly decaying, but he'd certainly been there. The creatures were curious about where this human had been. They were intensely curious about all things having to do with him, even though they were going to kill him the moment they found him.

The creatures weren't slowing for their own sake, though. They wanted instructions from their master.

The three didn't know him as the AllSeer or by any other name, for that matter. To them, he was the creator, the master, the beginning and end.

So they paused their voyage to see what he wanted them to do. It was the first time they had come across the target's DNA, even if only an aging bit of it. The creator might want them to go to it, or maybe they would be chastised for waiting.

It didn't take long for the creator's voice to reach them. The creatures spoke no language, but they'd been programmed to understand their master's will.

Go to it, he told them. *Destroy it.*

The creatures were blind to what was in the third dimension, at least from the fifth. They didn't know if they were heading to a world or a single corvette, nor did they care. The creatures didn't understand fear or the concept of defeat. They cut each other's limbs off for fun, and death was something they only recognized in others.

They dropped from the fifth to the fourth and finally to the third dimension without anything but a vague sense of curiosity.

A few hundred kilometers away, they saw the ship with their many eyes. Size and classification were beyond them, but they slowly flew through space, tasting the DNA as they went. It was growing stronger, and that increased their desire—nay, their *need.*

As the creatures sped up, the ship began to launch attacks at them. They easily slid away from the lasers that ripped through space at them, almost as if the weapons didn't exist.

Two smaller ships launched from the larger one.

The creatures paid them no mind. They sensed no DNA in the smaller ships, so they weren't important.

It wasn't until the ships discharged their lasers that two of the creatures looked at them. They came to an immediate halt, the three tentacles of each facing ships tens of kilometers off. After a brief second, they rushed toward them while the third creature continued toward the larger ship.

The corvettes tried to maneuver away from the black squid-looking things, but it was futile. Their lasers, their plasma weapons—they were all for nothing. Once the strange, never-before-seen beings reached the ships, their pilots died almost immediately.

The first creature to reach a corvette wrapped all three tentacles around the ship's viewport and squeezed. Metal, reinforced glass, and everything else crumpled beneath the immense pressure. The person inside stood no chance, dying without anyone hearing his scream.

The second creature was even quicker about its destruction. The corvette was trying to escape, flying in the opposite direction of the oncoming enemy. A dozen yards from the ship, the creature launched itself forward, all three of its tentacles spinning. It cut through the metal, shearing the ship into pieces.

The human inside was sucked out of the first opening, breaking limbs before his lungs exploded in his chest.

The metal parts of the ship whirled out into space's emptiness.

The two attacking creatures turned back to the main ship. Their counterpart had nearly reached it and was increasing its speed with each passing second, a type of bloodlust having come over it at being so near the target's DNA.

The remaining two chased it.

Lasers continued firing from the ship's cannons, but they just soared out into space, hitting nothing.

As the first creature neared the ship, it put its tentacles

together almost in a point. They sliced through the reinforced metal exterior as if it were wet paper. Space's vacuum ripped out people and objects alike, the cold reaching its long fingers in to freeze anything that remained standing.

The creature crashed through wall after wall, the vacuum protocols meant to save those deep in the ship pointless.

There were screams, cut short as the remaining two biomechanical weapons rushed into the ship.

There was joy, but only from the black-tentacled creatures. It was a joy very few humans would understand—the psychopaths perhaps, those who wanted more than anything to watch something beautiful burn.

At the destruction's end, frozen bodies and bent metal floated where a functioning ecosystem had once existed. The three creatures looked at their final product for a few seconds, once again feeling nothing but the need to continue toward the target's DNA.

There was no word from the creator, nor was there any need for it. They knew what to do.

They entered the fourth dimension, then the fifth, and began their flight once again.

The AllSeer knew his time on his planet was nearing an end. The war machine he'd started building a thousand years ago was in full swing now, things waking up that had been dormant for hundreds of years.

He watched as his three children destroyed the carrier.

It'd been easy and fun for them, so he hadn't minded letting them play a little. The AllSeer had spent time watching them during their flight, and he'd become more impressed the more he observed. Their single-minded search was exactly what he'd wanted when he'd begun their creation.

They would find the prophesied one; that he was sure of.

Unfortunately, the AllSeer was starting to wonder if they would be able to defeat him.

That was something he'd never thought he'd have to consider, at least not when he'd first unleashed them on an unsuspecting universe. He'd thought those formidable beings could kill a man, even one with the physical gifts of his sister's warrior.

Even if the AllSeer couldn't see like Alexandria, the AllMother, he wasn't blind. He'd been keeping up with the man's conquests and growing abilities.

This prophesied one was becoming more than strong. The AllSeer hadn't believed anyone would attempt to combine his own gifts with his sister's, but it appeared she'd done just that since the man had the physical powers the AllSeer's father had granted him. More and more, he was beginning to believe his sister had done the unthinkable.

He'd had a planet bow to him.

He'd conquered another one.

He'd united warlords.

Now, he was strong enough to begin his attempt to conquer the Commonwealth, or he thought he was. The AllSeer knew Kane was heading to the portal and that soon he'd put all of his people into the Commonwealth's solar system.

If his children couldn't stop him, the AllSeer would be forced to do it himself.

Already, his preparations were being made. He would wait, and within a few days, he'd know if his children could defeat the god-like creature.

He knew his sister still lived, though the woman had nearly killed herself fighting those warlords. The AllSeer couldn't reach out to her; her powers were too weak, and he couldn't make the connection without her cooperation, willing or unwilling.

No matter. She traveled with the prophesied one, and as long as the creatures understood that she was not to be harmed regardless of what happened, perhaps he would have her soon.

If not, he'd have her where it all began, and all these years later, a sort of madness having taken over Alexander de Finita, first of his name, he could still see the poetry in that.

CHAPTER FOUR

The Machine Planet
In Search of a Rumored Algorithm

Veena had been nine years old when her mother passed away. She had been twelve when her father died and she became a full-fledged orphan. She didn't have any siblings, so the loneliness that came to her wrapped around her like a second skin. Indeed, it covered her so tightly, she didn't even realize it existed. It wasn't loneliness, it was her *life*.

People came and went, but she'd never considered letting anyone in. Truthfully, it hadn't been a conscious decision but had happened beneath the surface of thought. Her parents' death had done something to her that she couldn't understand at twelve years old.

A coping mechanism? Probably.

For Veena, it had simply been a way to keep from hurting. If people didn't get close to her, then their removal from her life wouldn't hurt her. It might seem immature to an adult, but she'd been a child, and that was how her mind had dealt with what had happened.

You shut down the things that could rip you apart so you could make it through life. The alternative had been unbearable.

Boyfriends came and went. She'd even had a few lovers over the years, though every one of them had been kept at a distance. Children? Not a chance because to even consider losing progeny would have left Veena a weeping mess.

The Commonwealth. Duty. Primus. Those had been the things that gave her life meaning as an adult. As smart as Veena was, she had never gone very deep into her psyche. She had never dared consider why she had no friends, not truly. She had never dared consider why there'd not been a proposal or even a true suitor.

She didn't consider why she had a second skin made of loneliness, one that separated her from any real connections.

Veena was dreaming, not understanding where she was or what was happening around her. In her mind, she was back in that black box, the one floating in the middle of space. Ares had told her to leave, and she'd fled the room with the robots. She was making her way back to the ship, sure it wouldn't take off.

She knew she was going to die like Ares, but she had to try.

"Are you scared of death?"

It was her father's voice, which was odd for a lot of reasons. One, he was dead, and two, she never heard his voice. His or her mother's. Once they'd died, she'd cut them out like a surgeon would a cancerous chunk of cells. Letting those voices remain would have meant leaving a cancer in her psyche.

Veena stopped walking and impulsively turned the MechPulse so it crossed her chest, gripping it with both hands.

Her mother spoke next. "We didn't raise you long, but we didn't raise a coward, did we? I can't see you being scared of death, even though we're gone."

The voices came from behind her. Veena didn't want to turn around. She'd rather put the MechPulse to her head than see her deceased parents.

"Why are you running, Veena?" her dad continued. "You know you're not making it off this box. Death is in front of you, and death is behind you."

"You're going to die," her mother agreed.

"Are you scared of dying for someone else?"

The question hung in the air. Veena didn't want to answer it, and she didn't want to hear another syllable from her dead parents' mouths.

She heard footsteps behind her, soft ones—those of her mother.

The dead woman didn't touch her—and Veena thanked the gods for that, for she surely would have unleashed the pulse.

She did lean in, though.

"We didn't want to leave you, baby. You were the greatest joy of both our lives, and we would have stayed with you forever if we could have."

Veena heard her father's footsteps.

He was going to say something too. She could feel the air moving behind her to get closer to her ear.

Veena couldn't handle any more words, not from them. Whatever they had to say, they should have said it when they were alive. They'd lost their chance to speak to her.

Veena turned as quickly in her dream as in real life.

She spun, ready to kill her parents.

Her eyes opened then, and she found herself staring at the strangest-looking ceiling she'd ever seen.

Tears were rolling down her face.

***

Ares knew he was in a dream.

He knew it because he couldn't be fighting his father. He'd never do that, yet here he was, his Whip in his hand. His father stood across from him with a laser-saber.

They were beneath blue skies. Desert sand spread in all directions. Red sand. Ares had never been to this place, but he knew where it was: the desert on Mars.

It stretched for many kilometers, and Ares had only heard stories about it.

His father's eyes were cold. He held the saber across his chest.

"I'm not going to fight you," Ares whispered.

There was no wind, nothing to keep his words from reaching his father.

"Do you think you have a choice, son?"

Ares nodded. "I won't ever fight you. I love you."

"You'll die, then," Adrian responded.

Ares' Whip was at his side, and he dropped it to the

sand. The crimson lasers retracted into the hilt, and the weapon lay next to his feet. "That's okay. I love you. I won't fight."

His father's cruel eyes scanned the desert behind Ares. "Have you been here before? As a Titan, did you ever make it to this desert?"

Ares shook his head. He knew this was a dream, and apparently, his father did too. It was the oddest dream he'd ever had.

"You're going to end up here," his father said. "Soon." His eyes fell on his son. "You'll fight me, or you'll die. You'll kill me, or you'll die."

Ares shrugged. "I'll die then, Father."

"So be it."

Adrian was fast, even the dream version. Ares could have stopped him; his father wasn't so fast that Ares' natural speed couldn't stop him.

The former Titan did nothing.

He watched as the saber slashed through the air...

Ares' eyes opened.

He was lying on his back, staring at the strangest ceiling. He didn't know how long he'd been in here and waking up to it, though he knew this was the tenth time he'd dreamed.

The dreams were... Well, as he looked at the ceiling, he knew what they *weren't*: human. They were machine-made dreams, somehow implanted into his mind when he fell asleep, and he had a suspicion it had something to do with this ceiling.

If you stared at it too long, you could see anything.

Ares had tried touching it to understand if it was digital

or solid-state, but when his finger got close, a rough shock hit him. He only tried it once, then decided it didn't matter what the damn thing was made of.

Colors—every color imaginable—floated across it. Sometimes they swirled in a circle, moving inward like an inverted waterspout. Sometimes they floated over one another like clouds in a sky. Yet other times, the colors turned dark, and it looked almost like a storm was above him.

Ares imagined Earth had technology that could make ceilings looks like this, but he thought there was more to it.

He thought that somehow these machines were digging into his mind every time he fell asleep. He wasn't one to dream about his father, and when he did dream, he hardly ever remembered them. Dreams had made up very little of his life.

Yet now, he dreamed every single time he slept, and he remembered them perfectly.

Ares swung his feet off the bed and sat up—though bed was a relative term. It was more or less a cot bolted to the wall, though he had slept in much worse quarters.

He didn't know where Veena was. They'd been separated early on. Ares, wearing his MechSuit and retaining his Whip, had considered fighting, but Veena had told him not to.

He had no doubt that he could have deactivated quite a few of those machines, but in the end, they would both have died. He didn't think they'd hurt Veena any more than they'd hurt him. They could have, obviously, but he didn't think that was the point of them being here. At least, not the *machines'* point.

Ares didn't know where his Whip was, let alone the suit.

He stood up, dressed in clothing that looked like it might fall apart if a stiff wind blew on it. A little servant-like machine had delivered it before rolling somewhere else. Ares had given it a name. "Monk," though it didn't seem to understand anything he said to it.

He walked across the room to the wall, which was also the exit. This part of the machine world was much more technologically advanced than anything the Commonwealth had invented. It changed from opaque to transparent at different times, which wasn't anything special, but Monk could simply roll in through it. Ares had tried to leave while the machine rolled through, but he had run into a hard wall, causing his nose to bleed.

It didn't matter which part of the wall Ares tried to exit through; he found a barrier. The little machine bastard rolled right through, however.

Ares stretched his arms into the air. The wall was transparent now, and he could see what looked like similar cells. There were other creatures in them, none of them human and none of them resembling anything close to Earthborn animals. He had spent time trying to get the creatures to pay attention to him, to *hear* him, but all was for naught. None of the creatures looked at him, and none of them tried to make contact.

Either they had been here a long time and understood it didn't matter what they did, no communication would be forthcoming, or...

They didn't exist.

Ares was leaning toward the latter. The alien creatures

were simply too strange, as if they'd been made up from a story and not created by the gods or evolution.

Either way, it didn't matter. They weren't trying to speak to him.

Ares had dreamed ten times, but he didn't think that was because he'd been here for a long time. Rather, he thought the ceiling was making him sleep more. Something happened while he slept, and the machines were somehow using it.

He looked to the right down the white hallway. Monk was on the way. It came up to Ares' knees and rolled on treads. It had arms and hand-like instruments, though most of the time they held a serving tray with food or liquids or some new threadbare clothing.

As Ares watched it approach, he realized he was starting to humanize the thing and thinking of it as "he."

What does it matter? Ares thought. *I'm alone on a foreign planet, and this non-speaking entity is my only real company. I'll call him "he" if I damn well want to.*

Sometimes Monk rolled past Ares' cell and down the hallway to some other destination. This time, though, it rolled to a stop in front of the Titan.

It had no serving tray, and its body had straightened in a way Ares hadn't known was possible. He must have hunched the rest of the time, but now its head reached Ares' shoulder.

Monk's head was human-like. It had blue eyes on the front of its gray metal skull. Its nose poked out like a dog's rather than a human's, and there appeared to be a mouth on the end, though Ares had never heard a word come from it or seen the machine eat.

"How's it going, Monk?" Ares asked.

The machine did something different: it cocked its head to the left as if trying to understand his words. Usually Monk moved almost like a tank—a square thing that only looked straight ahead, but as it cocked its head, Ares was struck by how much the thing resembled a praying mantis.

"That's a new look for ya, Monk. I can't say whether I like it or not."

When the machine spoke, the voice was bass-filled and electrical. It wasn't close to human. "Come with me."

Ares' face showed no surprise, his father's training holding strong. He glanced at the four corners of the wall. "Ya know, Monk, if I wasn't smarter, I'd think you were trying to get me to bust my nose again. I remember that you didn't provide me with anything to wipe up the blood. Just this." He reached down and lightly pulled on the shirt. "And it doesn't soak up liquids very well."

"Your sense of humor is understood if unappreciated. Come with me, Romulus de Livius."

Ares wasn't surprised that the machine knew his name, though he did wonder how much the thing knew. There wasn't any use sitting here arguing with it, though. Rather than walk forward, he placed a hand on the wall, and for the first time, it wasn't solid.

It felt like he was sticking his hand through running water, even though the wall didn't appear to be moving. Ares pushed his hand all the way through, and he saw it on the other side.

"Well, damn, Monk, you aren't lying." Ares stepped through, the feeling of water running over him covering his body. He stepped to the other side and looked at his arms, then pushed his hair back, half-expecting it to be wet. He was dry, and the mantis-looking Monk was staring up at him.

"Come with me," he repeated in that bass-filled voice.

"Mind telling me where we're going?"

"It is time." Monk whirled then, and its treads started scooting it down the hall.

Ares didn't think about attacking the machine. Anything he did now besides listen to Monk would most likely result in pain if not death, yet before following, he did a quick look around. There were alien creatures in the two cells next to him and as far down as he could see.

He walked forward a few steps after Monk but stopped in front of the cell next to his.

A hybrid creature stared at him. From the neck down it looked wolfish, though it stood on two legs. From the neck up, it had pale skin, blue eyes, and an attractive human face.

"Come!" Monk boomed from in front of him.

"I'm coming, I'm coming," Ares said as he gazed at the hybrid.

He could probably stop in front of every cell and see something different, but right now, Monk was staring at him, and *its* blue eyes didn't seem too happy.

Ares moved forward, but Monk waited until he was a meter away before starting again.

"I came here with a woman, Monk, but I don't see her in any of these cells. Tall, not a bad figure, brunette. You know who I'm talking about?"

"You came here with another humanoid. She is still under observation."

They passed cell after cell, and Ares couldn't help but look at the different creatures. They were all fucking *strange*. "Look, we can get back to the humanoid, but are these things I'm looking at real?"

Monk stopped and whipped around so it was facing Ares. The movement was so sudden, the Titan almost ran into the machine, barely stopping in front of it. "Calm down, robot butler."

He had something else to say, but when he opened his mouth, he was dropping. It was fast enough that his feet rose off the ground, though the machine remained stationary.

Ares' hand shot forward and he grabbed Monk's metal arm to steady himself as walls whipped past him. If he leaned too far in one direction or the other, he'd be injured if not ripped apart.

He pulled himself close to the robot, realizing it could kill him without much trouble. His core was open to the creature, but there wasn't anything he could do about it.

"Calm," the machine said.

Ares' looked down at it with no emotion. "Don't I look calm, Monk?"

"Your father trained you well, but your pulse has risen. Remain calm or severe injury may occur."

That was one of the main differences between him and Alistair. Between Alistair and anyone, really. The man's body didn't react to outside stimuli.

Ares ignored the comment about his father. He understood they were in his mind, playing with his dreams, and hopefully he'd understand the purpose soon.

The hole they'd dropped through had closed. He could

only see the lights lining the tunnel. He turned his head to Monk, but the machine was staring forward as if it were out of commission.

The platform slowed, then it exited the tunnel.

It came to a stop and hovered just above the floor, about two meters from the ceiling. Ares thought about saying something smart, but as he turned around, the words fled his head.

A hundred—maybe two hundred—machines were on the floor. They were small rat-like things. They didn't have tails, but they rested on four metal legs and looked up at him with flat faces and red eyes.

Monk wasted no time. He rolled off the platform, nearly crunching five of the rat-machines. They rushed out of his way quickly, though he swiped with one of his arms and grabbed one. Monk tossed it behind him, his blue eyes growing brighter as he did.

If they're connected, Ares thought, *then they're communicating without speaking.*

He stepped off the platform. None of the rat-machines rushed him, but rather they left a path for him to follow Monk. As he moved forward, he looked behind him and saw that they were closing up and following. Some lashed out at the others that got too close, making them appear even more animal-like.

Monk was a few meters ahead of him, really booking it.

Ares jogged after him. "What are these things, Monk? Are they your rats?"

Monk said nothing, just kept rolling.

After another five minutes of following the machine while being followed by a bundle of them, Monk came to a stop. He didn't look at Ares but kept his head facing forward.

The rat creatures had halted much farther behind and formed a semi-circle.

"Go forward and focus your eyes on the panel," Monk told him.

Ares had come along without showing any apprehension, but he was done with the charade. All the machines were showing either fear or reverence toward the panel on the far wall; Ares couldn't tell which.

Either way, this behavior was different, and he didn't like it.

"What is it?" he asked the machine.

"Go forward and focus your eyes on the panel."

"What if I don't?"

The rats behind him chittered as if they understood the question.

Monk turned his head to the right while his body kept facing forward. "Your journey ends."

Ares didn't ask any more questions. Monk wasn't telling him he'd be put back on his ship and sent back to a world populated with humans. The journey Monk was talking about was life.

Fuck it, Ares thought.

He went forward. Monk's head turned to follow him.

The panel was built into the white wall, the only black on it. Ares was just about to bend over when the panel started moving up to his height. It slid up the wall; Ares didn't understand how that was even possible, but he would add it to the list.

The panel stopped in front of his face.

The lights dimmed.

Nothing else happened, though. There was no light from the panel, nothing that said it had scanned his eyes.

A few seconds passed, then Monk spoke from behind. "To the right."

Ares turned his head, and for the first time, he saw a technology he understood. It was an oldie but a goody. "Go in?"

"Yes," the machine responded.

"If I make it out of here, Monk, we're going to need to discuss putting some jokes in your programming. Some kind of levity. Your bedside manner needs work."

Ares went to the right. The rat-machines chittered, their voices high-pitched. Ares forced down the fear growing in him. He'd been a Titan, a Primus, and was still a de Livius, son of Adrian.

He turned the doorknob and pulled open the door.

Bright white light flooded out and blinded Ares to everything except its glory.

The white light was suddenly gone, and Ares found himself in his father's study.

It wasn't his present-day father, though, but the man who had told Ares not to lose his soul. That it was better to be low and have a soul than high and not have one.

His father sat behind his desk, looking at work in front of him, but instead of a DataTrack, paper sat on it—which didn't make any sense. Ares didn't think he'd ever seen actual paper for people to write on. Given the resources on this planet, he wasn't sure how it could be here, either.

Adrian looked up. His face was as measured and stern as it'd been years before. It was *almost* perfect, but it was missing something. Ares couldn't pinpoint it; he only knew this was a mere representation of his father.

"How long have I been in a simulation?" Ares asked, finally understanding what this was.

His father placed his pen on the desk. "The changeover happened after we separated you and your companion."

"It's all been a simulation? The cell, the other creatures I saw, the trip down here? I've been having dreams inside dreams, basically?"

Adrian leaned back in the chair. "That's a simplistic way of looking at it, but it'll work for now."

Maybe there'd be time to consider the technicalities of that at some point, but Ares had never been a man for pondering the world. He preferred to move through it, and that was what he needed to do now. "What is this place? Who built it?"

"If I told you I don't know, would you believe me?"

"No," Ares said. He looked to his left at where his father's window should be, then walked over to it and looked down. He saw the rolling hills he'd seen growing up. A brown horse was grazing. Ares turned his eyes to the sky. Large, puffy clouds slowly moved across it. "What are you?"

"You should think of me as a caretaker. I look after this place."

"The simulation or the actual world?" Ares knew machines ruled this planet. It wasn't all a simulation.

"Both. Simulations are primarily used to understand those who reach this planet."

"The others I saw in the cells? Simulations?" Ares asked.

"Representations of others who came. You will have a representation too."

The complexities in this place kept growing. Ares turned toward the desk. "Is Veena in the simulation? Is she okay?"

A slight nod. "She's okay."

"If you don't know where this place came from, why is it here? Is it the algorithm?"

Adrian stood and walked to the window. His gait and height were perfect, though *something* was still off.

Adrian looked out the window at the horse. "The algorithm is here. This world exists to house the algorithm. Everything here, including this simulation, is meant to protect it."

Ares shook his head. "That's not possible. The person who stole it sent it away without anyone knowing. Anyone who could create this place could fight the Commonwealth. Most likely win, as well."

"Your lack of knowledge is not surprising, but your belief in this anti-knowledge is astounding." He nodded at the window. "Look out there."

Ares turned his head, and he found himself staring into space. A single ship was floating in the distance, though not so far away that he couldn't make it out.

"That's the closest representation we could build of the original ship that contained the algorithm. Do you know how many people were aboard it?"

"I don't know anything about that ship or this place

except that there's supposed to be an algorithm. One that allows for an almost all-knowing AI and the ability to upload one's mind into the cloud. That's what I'm here for, that algorithm."

His father spoke as if he'd said nothing. "The ship found this place. I was already here, and I'd been waiting for it. There were three hundred and forty-two people on it when it arrived, though of course, they weren't allowed to leave. I did my best to make their remaining years as pleasant as possible. Obviously, some of them resented me, us, and this place, but there wasn't anything I could do about that."

The scene in front of Ares morphed to the ship landing on this barren planet, with humans exiting the dreadnought. Ares had stopped watching, though, turning his head toward Adrian. "You were waiting for it?" he asked. "Meaning, you knew it was coming?"

Again, his father didn't give a response to what Ares had said. "Since then, almost one thousand years ago, others have come here. Many more than you saw in those simulated cells. All have failed to get the algorithm. My programming told me that one would come, but my programming also allows me to learn through my experiences. I had begun to believe that no one would appear. That I would guard the algorithm forever."

The image in the window turned black.

Ares stepped away from it, moving to the far wall. "Everything you're saying is insane. Your circuits are frying because none of this is possible. *If* I believe the notion that the ship landed here, there isn't any way you were waiting for it. Most likely, the algorithm was reprogrammed by someone who came later to bring us, after building you, and for what reason, I can't imagine. For you to be waiting for it, either the gods or someone from the future would have had to set all this up."

To Ares' surprise, his father nodded solemnly. "My only question is, would there be any difference between someone from the future or a god? To you, to me, only able to travel one way through time, wouldn't such a being look the same?" He paused for a second. "What do you want the algorithm for?"

"You've lived in my mind. Don't you know?"

"You're the first from your solar system to come here." He turned from the window to look at Ares. "Why did you come here to get this algorithm?"

Ares fixed his jaw and stared at the representation of his father. "What else was I going to do? I gave up everything. I'm a hunted man. That algorithm is worth more than my and Veena's lives times a thousand. Ten thousand. If we get it, we can buy our freedom."

His father looked at the floor. "I can count how many have come here, wanting credit or money, whatever term they use for currency. It's a high number, Romulus de Livius. A higher number come to use the algorithm to build their own machine. Truthfully, everything I've done was to ensure those people don't get it."

"Why are we talking?" Ares asked. "You know me as well as I know myself. What is the point of this?"

Adrian looked up, and Ares finally understood what was different about the thing.

It was the eyes.

His father was stern, even cold, but there was love in

the man. Behind the hard eyes and the stiff upper lip, a certain kind of love drove him.

This representation couldn't replicate that. It couldn't put love behind those eyes, no matter how much it knew.

"I'm only the keeper of the algorithm. I don't own it, and I was never supposed to. You and I are talking because I wanted to speak to the ones who would lift this burden from me and those who helped protect the algorithm."

"I don't understand. I'm going to buy my life with it, and I haven't even considered who I'll sell it to. Maybe it'll be one of those who want to build their own intelligence."

The representation smiled, though even then, it couldn't fake love. "Your lack of knowledge isn't surprising, but your belief in it is still astounding. We're well met, Romulus de Livius."

Ares opened his mouth to speak again about how little sense any of this made, but the simulation began to fall apart.

His body, the body of his father, the room around them —they all started to flake apart in perfect squares.

Ares couldn't speak, and then he couldn't see.

His universe went black.

CHAPTER FIVE

Eight weeks of the sham marriage had gone by, and shockingly, Luna wasn't dead. She hadn't thought they'd make it three days, but each day, she found herself going through the motions. At night they lay together; he made his lovemaking moves beneath the covers, and she moaned softly. They never touched outside of cheek against cheek; the beast hadn't lied. He wouldn't take her against her will. When he faked his orgasm, she rolled over on her side and lay crying without sound, wondering when this would all end.

Yet, Luna kept going, and she came to see the beast named Hector as a better man than the Ascendant. Luna felt nothing like love or even lust for him, only grudging respect. She knew she was beautiful, and for a man to lay next to her each night and never once try touching her outside of their fake sex? Well, it took honor to do that.

Luna was coming to see that she lived in a world without much honor. The men she'd once thought of as near-gods were scrambling ants trying to keep their spot in the hill, nothing more.

Despite the respect, she was almost overwhelmingly relieved when Hector told her he was leaving. Luna's face couldn't show that relief, and it took everything in her to keep from collapsing.

She sat down, then crossed one leg over the other before folding her hands over one knee. "When will you be back?"

Hector was sipping a glass of water. He rarely looked at her when they were together but kept his huge body turned half away. "I'm not sure. However long it takes, I suppose."

"Where are you going?" Luna asked. She had two concerns here, the most immediate being how long they would be separated. She desperately wanted...nay, *needed* time away from this man. Respect or not, she wasn't meant to live with anyone besides Alistair.

The second concern dealt with him—Allie, her true husband. She knew this monster-sized man had come here for war. Hector had shared some things with her, as would be expected of a spouse. Alistair was alive and bringing war to the Commonwealth. Luna surprised herself by not caring a bit about what happened to the government she'd grown up under. When she heard what Alistair was doing, all that mattered was that she might see him again.

The beast had come to kill her true husband. That was his reason for being here, so where he was going mattered greatly.

"We're fairly certain we know which portal Kane is heading to," Hector answered. "His force is too big to hide, and given his current trajectory, we know the planet he'll use to get back to our solar system. We plan on stopping him at that planet so there's no chance he can cause harm to us at home."

He placed his glass on the counter.

"I'll be back when that job is done."

Luna's breath caught in her lungs. "You're going to kill him?"

Hector nodded. "I'm going to do everything I can to protect the Commonwealth. I'll kill him there, and then we can return to Mars."

"I wish you luck, my husband," Luna managed to say.

She couldn't hold back anymore, and Hector must have known it was coming.

He reached into his jacket pocket, pulled out the black orb, and set it on the counter next to his empty glass. He pressed the button on top and left the room as the tears started running down Luna's face.

She tried to cover her face with her hands. Her body doubled over so her elbows were on her knees.

Luna had lived with this man—Hector—for almost two months, and she understood Alistair had no chance against him. It didn't matter how great a Titan Alistair had been. This man was *inhuman*. He would kill her husband, and there wasn't anything she could do about it.

She had to sit here while it happened.

The sobs caused her shoulders to shake and her back to heave. She cried loudly, knowing that for the moment, no one would hear her pain. She could let it out.

Luna cried for her marriage and her husband.

She prayed for the gods to intervene.

She prayed for Hector's death, the Ascendant's, everyone involved with this thing against Alistair.

In the end, when her tears had dried and her body was drained, nothing had changed. All her rage, all her sadness… It was the same.

Her husband was going to die, and there was nothing she could do to stop it.

Hector pitied the woman. He wouldn't lie to her since he thought she deserved better than that. *He* was better than that. She was a strong woman who had been placed in a horrific position, one she hadn't been prepared for. Despite him coming from an even more privileged background than she had, his life had been very different. Harder. He'd faced hardships and seen death from an early age.

He'd watched friends lose limbs and have their entrails fall on the ground, their stomachs opened by a laser.

Hector could do nothing to help her. The best he could do was give her space to let the anguish come out, but even that couldn't last long. He'd have to go get the stealth machine shortly, and then it would be time for him to leave.

Hector could hear her crying in the main room, but he pushed her sorrow from his mind and went back to the conversation he and his grandfather had just had.

Hector had left much of that conversation out of what he'd told Luna. He was going to a distant planet to defend the Commonwealth, but he hadn't told her which planet or what waited there.

Phoenix.

That was the planet's name, the Terram people having named it for the flames that made up the atmosphere. They had sworn their allegiance to this Alistair Kane, and all reports said the former Titan planned to use it to return to the Commonwealth.

Therefore, the Ascendant would kill those sworn to him before killing *him*.

Hector wasn't leading the army, he was only a member of it, but that was fine. That was what his grandfather wanted, and Hector believed Caius was right. It was better to keep a low profile, and when the war came, let his deeds speak for him. His accomplishments would push him up the ranks. No one would be able to deny the genius he'd displayed on the battlefield.

The woman's crying was loud, piercing his thoughts. Hector didn't mind her showing her pain, but he didn't appreciate the interruption.

He stepped out onto the bedroom's balcony, and the door closed behind him. He looked out at the garden.

Hector understood the Ascendant knew nothing of hardships either. He lived in this residence, surrounded by everything he could ever want. Hector knew the story of Aurelius de Finita, the first Imperial Ascendant. *He* had gone through true hardships to create this empire. Those after him? Some yes, some no, but Alexander de Finita, the second of his name, lived like a fat Roman emperor.

Hector felt no pity for what would soon befall the man. His grandfather thought the Ascendant was more clever than Hector. Where the grandson saw weakness, Caius saw cunning. As always, Hector would defer to his grandfather, but when war came, as it soon would, the weakness would be revealed.

Which brought him to Alistair Kane.

The Commonwealth had gotten holovids of the man, and Hector had spent the past eight weeks studying them nightly. After Luna was asleep, he rose from the bed and watched the man fight. Hector wouldn't lie to himself and say he wasn't impressed. Kane moved differently than anyone Hector had ever seen, including him. He seemed to be everywhere at once, yet no blows fell on him. He'd watched the battle with the woman, shocked by the sheer heart Kane had shown.

It'd been as if he'd wanted to lose, but in the end, he couldn't let himself.

More, the Commonwealth had captured holovids of his mental abilities, if that was what they were. Caius had told Hector they were a product of his mutation, and Hector knew the rumors about Alexandria de Finita, the supposed AllMother.

None of that mattered, though. The difference between him and the former Titan was primarily in the man's mental powers. While Kane was physically impressive, Hector knew he could kill him. No man was his equal in war. No mutant, either.

Hector took a deep breath and leaned against the rail.

Tomorrow he left for Phoenix. They weren't able to travel by portal. The Terram had shut down the portal, so they'd be traveling in the fourth dimension for much of the way.

The estimates showed they'd arrive about two weeks before Kane. The former Titan couldn't go into the fifth dimension with humans at his side, so there wasn't much he could do to speed up his travels. He would know Phoenix was being attacked and not be able to do anything about it.

Alexander had no shortage of warriors. He had no shortage of Primuses. The Commonwealth had bred them since his ancestor first created the empire, and that tradition had continued.

What he did have a shortage of was loyalty. People he could trust, as Caius had shown with his monstrosity of a grandson. Even now, Alexander's people were trying to reverse-engineer how he'd mutated Hector without his eyes appearing red. They would know the answer soon, though Alexander didn't plan to use that publicly against Caius.

A shortage of loyalty; that was his problem.

Alexander stood with his back to the orb, his arms locked onto each other at the small of his back.

"It seems you now understand the danger," the Fathers said as one.

"And it seems you missed the freak of nature Caius brought to Earth. Yet another threat to my rule."

The orb chuckled. "That freak of nature might be the thing that saves the Commonwealth."

Alexander understood the Fathers were mocking him, but he didn't take the bait. "I'm sure Caius would love to keep your uploaded selves around when he takes over." He turned to look at the small dot in the middle of the large orb. "I don't have time for this back and forth. In the morning, we leave for Phoenix. I've given you a hundred soldiers, and I need to know who you think I can trust. Do you have recommendations for me or not?"

Alexander had uploaded the dossier of the hundred people an hour before. It should have been finished immediately, but the Fathers wanted to chastise him more. Alexander could hardly imagine uploading himself into the orb with them and spending the rest of eternity next to such nagging pissants.

"We've sent back the top three candidates," the orb responded. "The probability of trusting any one of them is below ninety percent, but we find the female you sent over has the greatest opportunity."

Less than ninety percent? Were the gods against Alexander?

He swallowed, nodding. "Do you think I should involve her?"

"It depends on the nature of the mutant."

"Explain," Alexander said.

"The woman is loyal to the Commonwealth, but not you specifically. She follows you because you are the Commonwealth, but if she sees this Titan as a threat and that the best chance of survival is Hector de Gracilis, your hold on her will loosen."

"Thank you," he said, and despite his annoyance, once again went to his knees and bowed to the orb. "I'm going to stop him."

"Go to the woman," the orb commanded, "but remember, Alexander, you must make her see that the Commonwealth's true power rests with you."

Alexander's head remained bowed. "Is there anything else?"

"The chances of you stopping him at this portal are slim. We foresee Kane making it back here, and there will be another to contend with then."

Alexander knew who they were talking about: the first of his name, Alexander de Finita. The AllSeer.

"It isn't a myth," the orb continued. "The probability of the first still living is almost a certainty, as well as his sister. Your failure to contain this early has dramatically increased the chance that he will be returning to our solar system as well." The light moving across the orb condensed to a dot as it quit speaking.

"What does he want?" Alexander asked.

"We have no insight into his mind. Most likely, he is insane and devoid of any logic outside a destructive hunger. He'll bring fire and ash to us; that's all we can be sure of."

CHAPTER SIX

Petra de Osimian's hair was shaved almost to her skull. She had an extremely short crop over her dome, and the reason for cutting it so had nothing to do with vanity. She wasn't trying to start a new look within the Titans.

She wore it that short because if she was ever to fight without a helmet, there would be nothing for her enemies to grab.

There'd been no official measurement, but Petra was most likely the smallest of all the Titans. Perhaps the smallest Titan ever, not in height but in weight and body structure. She would have looked more at home in a ball-gown than in a MechSuit, though she'd never felt comfortable in fancy garments.

Currently, she was flying in a transport to a place she'd never been or ever thought she'd go. Petra had graduated from the Academy two years prior, and while she'd been in competition for First Graduate, she'd ended up losing to the man who most thought would end up as Primus someday. Even a Primus wasn't often brought to the Imperial

Residence, though, yet here she was being whisked away to it the night before an invasion began.

Petra had been told very little. She'd received a holovid message telling her to be ready in ten minutes, that a transport would pick her up. When she asked where she was going, the answer had changed everything: to meet with Alexander de Finita.

This was the largest offensive Petra had heard about in recent history, and although they were only loading up on dreadnoughts tomorrow, she wasn't going to be able to sleep much.

Now she wouldn't be able to sleep at all.

It was just after midnight, and the transport was quickly descending to a landing zone on the Imperial Residence's premises. Petra watched as land-to-air weapons followed the vessel's progress, ready to blast it and her out of the sky if the credentials it'd used to enter turned out to be false.

The transport touched down and was put into sleep mode. The side door opened and Petra stepped out. One of the legendary Praetorian Guard stood in front of her. In his MechSuit, he looked like a giant, and Petra found herself awed. She knew it was silly, given that she was a Titan, but all of the important public events in her short life had involved these men and women—the Praetorians.

"*Salve*, Petra," the guard said formally. "Please follow me. The Ascendant is waiting for you."

The guard turned, and in a walk that matched his formal speech, led her through the residence. Petra had developed skills other Titans didn't have, and she'd done it without noticing it was happening. Those skills were necessary for someone her size if she was to succeed in a world dominated by bigger men and women. As an example, she never actively paid attention to her surroundings, but she saw everything.

As she moved through the residence, her eyes never veered to the left or right, but her mind tallied every possible threat and every guard she saw. She found the exits, the stairways, and the elevators while her eyes remained focused on the back of the guard in front of her. Anyone watching would have no idea that Petra had just created blueprints in her mind of every room she traveled through.

She'd heard about the throne room and silently hoped she would be able to see it. That wasn't where the guard took her, though.

He led her to the gardens.

Petra had heard of the gardens as well, though she now realized the descriptions had failed to do it justice.

The Praetorian stopped just outside the entrance. Petra didn't look up or around, but she didn't need to. She saw it all at once, even as her mind focused on the face that had filled the millions of holovids she'd watched over the years. The face of the Commonwealth.

Alexander de Finita.

"Come in," the Ascendant called.

He sat in the middle of an enclosure. His body was thin, his limbs long, his face narrow. A bottle of what looked to be wine sat on a round glass table. An empty chair was on the far side of the small table.

Petra walked in. Glass walls surrounded her, with green and blue lights shining on the other side. The fifth Imperial

Ascendant had built this room and created the saltwater reef. Fish of all shapes, sizes, and colors moved through it. Crustaceans, squid, and other animals Petra couldn't begin to identify were clinging to corals or floating gently through the water.

Petra didn't look at the wildlife, but without a doubt, the aquarium was the most beautiful thing she'd ever seen.

She stopped just before reaching the table, her hands at her sides, her eyes straight ahead—a soldier.

"My ancestor was trying to be humorous when he named this place," the Ascendant said. "He called it 'the gardens' because he thought it would be funny to see his propraetors' faces when they walked in and saw it was a garden of the sea. Rather than humorous, it came off as arrogant."

De Finita picked up the glass in front of him and took a sip of the purple liquid.

"I rarely come here. It's probably been years since I was here last, yet no matter how long I stay away, the internal workings of this palace keep going. Someone—or an AI—monitors the PH and salinity. The feedings continue. The cleaning of the tank. All so that when I walk in here, I can see its beauty."

Petra had no idea what to say. She saw that the bottle looked to be one-fourth full and found no glass except the Ascendant's on the table.

He finally turned to look at her—not his whole body, but his head over his shoulder. "They tell me you hold the Commonwealth in deep reverence. Is that true?"

Petra's face showed no emotion, but she nodded. "Yes, my liege."

The Ascendant motioned at the empty chair. "Sit with me."

The Titan walked over to the chair, unsure of anything that was happening right now. It was already pulled out for her, and she sat down. She met de Finita's eyes. The lights from inside the tank revealed their faces to each other, if in a soft fashion. To Petra, he looked tired and slightly tipsy, though she didn't know him well enough to say that was the case.

"Would you like some wine?" he asked. "I can have them bring more."

"No, my liege."

"The dossier on you says you don't drink. That's true?" His voice was soft, but she could hear it well enough.

"Yes, sir."

"Why not?"

Petra had spoken to superior officers before; she knew the protocol for answering questions, even personal ones. She'd never been questioned by someone *this* high up, though, or been asked such a deep question. Did she tell him about her father's problems with alcohol as a young man? Did she talk about the allure of it for her—something that seemed dark and forbidding but that she wanted all the same?

The man was waiting for an answer.

"Someone my size needs every possible advantage in battle, my liege. Alcohol can dull the wits and slow the body. I mean no disrespect to your majesty by saying such things."

The Ascendant smiled and looked at the bottle of wine. "None taken. I don't usually drink this much, but it has been quite a day. Quite a month, really." He paused for a moment and didn't look up from the bottle when he continued. "Your dedication to the Commonwealth. Has anyone ever asked you about it? Have you ever talked about it with anyone?"

An odd question, but then, nothing about this encounter was what she'd call normal. "There were a few self-psychology tests given in the Academy. I've spoken to my parents and brother about it as well, but that's it."

He picked up his wine glass and gently swirled the liquid. "I brought you here because I wanted to hear about it. Why do you hold the Commonwealth in such high regard, Petra?"

He sipped his wine and set the glass down, then his eyes fell on her. They didn't look tipsy anymore. To Petra, they looked like they could see through her.

That gaze forced her answer out almost immediately. "The Commonwealth is what separates us from animals, my liege. Without the Commonwealth..." She dropped her eyes, staring down at the table and remembering what she knew of the past. "War, hunger, disease, hate—all of it existed in quantities we don't see today. Is there still murder? Of course. Hate? Yes, it still exists. Nothing can completely eradicate the dark side of humanity, but the Commonwealth has made the largest steps of any organization I've ever seen."

She looked up, unsure if she'd gone too far.

The Ascendant was looking at her with narrowed eyes. He twirled his fingers, obviously aware that she had more to say on the subject.

"'Demockracy' destroyed nations. The monarchs were

never strong enough or wise enough to take care of their people long-term. Every government failed eventually. Even the Roman Empire can't be compared to ours, my liege. If it took a month to pass a message, the Commonwealth has lasted a thousand times as long as they did. Maybe a million times." She swallowed. "The Commonwealth is humanity's first and last light."

The penetrating look disappeared and the Ascendant smiled. He tipped his glass toward her slightly, the purple liquid moving closer to the lip. "I'm not sure I could have said it better, Petra." He placed the glass down and looked at the tank. Petra followed his gaze. "Everything I do, everything I've ever done, it's all been to keep the Commonwealth safe. Perhaps the only way I would differ in my explanation is that the Commonwealth isn't just the government, it's the people too. Protecting them from their worst instincts, as well as from foreign enemies, has been my life's work.

"I have something I'd like to ask of you, and I was going to do it now, but the wine has made me too talkative. I know you have a big day ahead of you tomorrow, but would you spare me a few more moments?"

Feeling a bit freer to speak than when she first arrived, Petra blurted the answer. "I may never get another chance to be in front of you, my liege. If you'd like me to listen, nothing could pull me away."

"Thank you." He pursed his lips. "My upbringing was different than anyone else's to ever live, except for the male heirs in the de Finita lineage..."

CHAPTER SEVEN

That was what the people who wanted his throne didn't understand. They hadn't dedicated the time to earn it. Even Caius, with his enhanced mutant grandson, hadn't invested what Alexander had. Perhaps as an adult he'd grown complacent, maybe even weak by his ancestors' standards, but that didn't mean he hadn't trained his entire life for what was coming.

He had.

It didn't matter what the Fathers said or how they scoffed during their meetings.

Alexander knew what he'd grown up under, and he knew the ones who wanted the throne hadn't.

The story he told Petra de Osimian was one that had taken place when he was eleven years old. His father would have been about fifty since the de Finita males had their children late, spending the early years of their lives establishing their rule.

Alexander's father's name was Tessius, and he still missed the man. True, he could go speak with his uploaded consciousness or a version of it, but not alone. The others would be there too.

Tessius had been hard, harder than anyone ever knew. Alexander's mother had accepted her role when she took Tessius' hand in marriage. The raising of Alexander would be done under his father's strict guidance and all-seeing vision.

Nothing took place within Tessius' domain that he didn't have direct knowledge of. Much of Alexander's day-to-day instruction was given by teachers other than his father. He hadn't been trained to use the legendary Whip or learned history and advanced mathematics. He was a polymath and a fine physical specimen in his own right.

Yet his father always took time with him.

They had gone to the beach that week on what was supposed to be a vacation. His father took one each year, and they usually went to the same place. It was across the Atlantic ocean, and their house resided on a beautiful cliff that looked over the water. At the cliff's bottom, a beach waited, and in the evenings, their small family would go down to it.

Those were some of the sweetest memories Alexander had. For a few moments, his father forgot everything or appeared to and they were simply a family.

Most of the time.

The day he told Petra about, the rain was coming, and it would be a hard storm. Dark clouds danced overhead, and the wind was whipping the grassy lawn as if it were angry. In the distance, Alexander could see lightning touching down on the ocean.

He was outside, sitting in a chair a few feet from the

cliff. It was about time to go in, he knew that, but he wanted to study a bit longer. Alexander took his studies seriously, even at that young age, and he wanted to read his papers one more time. He would have a verbal test when they returned home, and he knew Professor Alrain wouldn't care where he'd been.

Alexander stood up to leave, and the wind ripped the papers from his hand.

His hands shot out to grab them, but the wind was too strong. He watched as all hundred sheets rushed higher than he could jump, then tumbled over the cliff.

He stepped forward and watched them streaming toward the sand, caught in a wind tunnel. It'd been his father who'd insisted he use paper and not a DataTrack, saying paper helped the mind learn better.

Now the paper was scattered, and rain was coming.

As he turned, knowing he would have to tell his father, it started to fall. Big fat wet drops hit his head.

He reached the porch door and went inside. His father was sitting on a couch, a DataTrack in his lap.

Alexander opened his mouth to say something, but his father spoke first. "Do you understand what you just did?"

"I lost my studies," the boy answered.

Thunder ripped through the outside air, loud and cracking.

"Do you know the work that goes into creating the paper you use, Alexander? You're privileged in ways you won't understand until you're older. Countless man-hours are spent so you can have the very best because one day, mankind's hopes are going to rest on your shoulders." Tessius finally looked up, his face lean like all the de Finita men. "You were careless with that paper, waiting too long to come back in. You were careless with those man-hours spent on you, and you were careless with the future of our people."

Alexander's eyes didn't fill with tears, nor did his face quiver.

His father continued, "I shut the elevator down for maintenance earlier today. You don't have any copies of those papers, do you?"

Alexander shook his head.

"Go get them, son. Hurry before they're lost. Other people can be careless, but a de Finita can't. Your future as well as humanity's is down there on those papers." With that, his father turned back to the DataTrack.

Alexander knew he had a choice. His father wasn't the type to command, yell, or rage. He'd given him an instruction and the reasoning behind it, but if he decided to remain in the house, Tessius wouldn't mention it again.

A de Finita didn't follow orders because he didn't need to. A de Finita was the most disciplined of men as well as the wisest.

Alexander's discipline forced him back out into the storm.

The rain hit so hard it stung. The waves were growing larger, and the wind?

Alexander understood it was hopeless. That the papers, if they weren't floating in the white-capped waves, were soaked or had ripped apart on rocks.

Alexander understood what his father had meant when he'd said the elevator was out of service. There was only one other way down: the cliff face.

He started running across the lawn, heading toward the shortest part of the cliff face he knew of. He knew how to rock-climb; he'd trained on it for years, but usually one had ropes, pulleys, and supports.

None of that existed now.

He made his way down as fast as he could. The strength of the wind was growing with each passing minute, but Alexander couldn't focus on or worry about that. He had to concentrate on each piece of drenched rock he touched.

The rain beat on him so hard he could barely see.

Ten feet from the bottom, he lost his grip.

The fall wasn't long, but he landed on his back, which knocked the wind out of him. Thunder roared across the sky as blood dripped from a gash across his forehead. He'd broken his left arm in the fall. The pain was excruciating, and at first, combined with the lack of oxygen, he couldn't compartmentalize it all.

After sixty seconds or so, Alexander was able to focus again. He shoved the pain down, almost able to disconnect it due to his training. He got to his feet and looked across the wind-swept beach. He saw no papers. He could hardly see anything, the rain was so thick.

Alexander never glanced at the cliff or where his home resided atop it. He understood his duty. He went forward into wind that knocked him down from time to time.

He searched up and down the beach, venturing into the water.

For hours and hours, he looked. The storm grew worse and lightning lit the night sky, but the young man didn't shirk his task. Tessius never came down to look for him, not even as the light grew brighter in the distance, the sun making its presence known.

The storm finally passed, and Alexander stood bleeding, broken, and exhausted at the bottom of the cliff. He knew what was required of him. He had to climb back up, but he also knew there was no way his arm would support him. He couldn't do it with only three limbs, which meant he'd failed.

A small *ding* came from the cliff's elevator. Alexander could just see it from where he stood; the door was open. It would only occur to him much later that maybe the elevator had not been out of service.

Alexander stumbled across the sand toward it. He'd lost one shoe when a wave had unexpectedly crashed down on him, and he had discarded the other at some point.

No one met him at the elevator; it was empty, waiting for a single occupant. Alexander stepped inside, and the door closed.

His muscles shook as he ascended to the house. He'd never been so tired in his life.

Finally, Alexander reached the lawn and stepped out of the elevator. He slowly walked to the porch and then inside the house. His father was in the same position he'd been when Alexander had left.

The Imperial Ascendant didn't look up from his Data-Track. "Did you retrieve them?"

Alexander swallowed, knowing he'd failed. "I found fifty-two."

"Out of how many?" his father asked.

"A hundred."

Tessius looked up, though he wasn't facing his son. He

nodded with pursed lips. "Your carelessness lost quite a few. I think you injured your arm as well, and you'll need to get it looked at immediately. Those are more resources that will need to be spent because of your carelessness, Alexander." His father finally turned to meet the boy's eyes. He held all the papers he'd found in his right hand. They were torn, dirty, and bent, but he held them just the same. "You messed up, but you did the best you could to make things right. In some ways, those papers are like humanity. Your carelessness can put them in danger, Alexander, but some of those papers wouldn't be found if I sent a team out there after them. Some papers will always be lost, and some of our people will too."

Tessius stood up then. He didn't hug his son or offer condolences. "Go to the med-room and have that looked at. I hope you learned your lesson."

Alexander had.

CHAPTER EIGHT

The Imperial Ascendant finished speaking. He tapped the side of his glass, staring at it. He was quiet for a long moment, and Petra didn't dare interrupt the silence.

"I've never told anyone that story. You're the first and most likely will be the last."

Petra was surprised by her next question. "Why?"

De Finita didn't look up, only kept tapping his glass. "Because of what I'm going to ask you to do."

"What's that?"

He glanced at her. "You've met your commander for the coming invasion?"

"Yes, my liege."

The Ascendant turned so that he faced her and moved the glass of wine to the side of the table. "His name is Hector de Gracilis. His grandfather is Caius de Gracilis. You've heard of him, yes?"

"One of the greatest Titans ever to live, and the first to jump to propraetor," she answered.

"That's right. What I'm going to tell you next, Petra,

cannot be repeated. Only I am privileged to know this information, so if it spreads, there's only one person I'm going to look at for an explanation. Do you understand?"

Petra nodded. She understood what he was saying. She wasn't sure she wanted to hear it, though. She wasn't sure she wanted to hear any more about any of this—not his history, not the future. She only wanted to be a soldier.

None of that mattered, apparently. Life had other plans for her.

"Caius and his grandson Hector are plotting to overthrow me."

Petra couldn't hold back her surprise. Her eyes widened, and her hands gripped her thighs. The Ascendant nodded, noticing her shock.

"It won't be a violent *coup d'état*, at least not in the beginning. Caius has been planning this for long years, and only now has he shown his final card: the mutant Hector." He took a deep breath and slowly let it out. "What I'm asking you to do, Petra, is be at his side all the time. I want to know what he does, when he does it, how he thinks, and anything that could relate to them overthrowing the Commonwealth."

"Hector?" Petra asked, feeling stupid the second the word left her mouth.

The Ascendant nodded again. "There are a few details you should know before you decide to accept this. I've arranged for you to be his capo, his second in command. He's going to suspect you of being my plant, but there's not a lot that can be done about that. He'll be surrounded by his own warriors for the most part, Mars born and bred. I won't say it won't be dangerous for you because I imagine if they find out you're a scout for me, an accident might befall you. Do you understand?"

"I think so," Petra replied.

"If you do accept this assignment, you'll be doing the Commonwealth a great service. We are facing the greatest threat since its inception, and risking a coup at the same time would be too much for the pillars of our government to withstand. If you accept this task, you'll help hold those pillars together."

Petra's mind was rapidly assimilating everything she was being told. At first, it'd been hard to take everything in. "May I ask how often you'll need me to report, my liege?"

"As often as necessary." Any trace of the tipsiness he'd shown in the beginning was gone. "At least once a week, and in the beginning, perhaps once every few days. I am relatively certain he's using stealth technology to block his conversations, though I can't accuse him of it yet. You'll be the Commonwealth's way around that."

"May I ask why someone would want to overthrow you, my liege?"

The Ascendant leaned back in his chair and tilted his head to watch the glass tank. After a few moments, he shrugged. "Everyone wants more power. It's in our nature to accumulate more. Perhaps Caius thinks he could rule better than me? He probably does because everything looks easier to the man watching. Only those performing know how hard it is to achieve every day. In the end, I guess it's that simple." He met her eyes. "In my position, I tell no one everything. I'm the only one who holds all the knowledge of the Commonwealth. I tell very few most things. Tonight you have been elevated to a level almost no one else will ever reach. It is both a privilege and a duty to know such things. The reason they want the throne is that they think they could do my job better, and they want to accumulate more power for their families. Do you have any other questions, Petra?"

She felt like the entire night had been rushed and her whole life had changed in a matter of seconds. She'd been prepared to die over the next few weeks because of the threat the former Titan posed. Now she was being told that another threat existed *inside* the Commonwealth, and she was being asked to…

Help the Commonwealth.

Only one question came to her mind at that moment, though later, there would be many more. For now, she could only think of a single important possibility. "Will I be tasked with killing him?"

"Would that be a problem?"

Petra thought for a few seconds as she held the Ascendant's gaze. "No." She shook her head. "Not if he's a threat to the Commonwealth."

"I doubt you'll be in that position," he responded. "If it comes up and you can do it safely, then perhaps I'll ask it of you…depending, as you said, on how great a threat he poses to the Commonwealth. Do you have anything else you'd like to ask? I want to make sure all your questions have been answered, Petra. It's very important you go into this with clear eyes."

She couldn't think of anything, so she shook her head. "No, my liege."

"Then will you accept this assignment from your Imperial Ascendant? Will you help protect the Commonwealth at all costs?"

Petra stood from her chair and walked to the other side of the table. She took a knee, bowing her head as she did. "I'll do as you wish, my liege. My life for the Commonwealth."

It was perhaps the most honest act Alexander had ever performed to hold onto his power. He'd leveled with someone so far below him that for her even to get a meeting with him was nearly unthinkable. Yet, the Fathers hadn't been wrong in their estimation of the woman. She was loyal to the Commonwealth, if not directly to him, and that was why he'd been so honest.

If she was to understand that he was the only man who could steer the Commonwealth through the coming war and its aftermath, she had to know some of how he'd prepared. He'd only given her one story, but there were a thousand more. Truthfully, there were an unlimited number he could give her if that was what she needed to understand that loyalty to him was paramount to saving the Commonwealth.

The bottle of wine was finished and Alexander was alone in the gardens, feeling slightly buzzed.

He stared at the fish and the coral without seeing them.

One thing he hadn't told the woman was another difference between him and those who wished for his throne: he would do anything to keep it. Had he not proven that to

Caius? His grandson could be forgiven for not understanding, but the propraetor? He wondered if the man wasn't going soft in the head as he grew older. Yes, Caius had obviously started his little revolution decades ago, but didn't he now know that Alexander would do anything to remain on the throne?

Perhaps now that the grandson was married to the former Titan's wife, Caius would see it.

Alexander sighed, alone with only animals to keep him company. Animals with memories that lasted only seconds that relied on instinct to make their next decision. The outside world might condemn his choices if they knew them, but none understood the strength it took to command humanity through a crisis.

None would want to know, either.

Caius and Hector would have to die, just as Kane would —and the AllSeer too, the one also named Alexander. Four who wanted his throne, and none who deserved it. None who had earned it.

Soon all four would go through the same trials Alexander had, and all four would die.

CHAPTER NINE

Alistair hated his current place in the universe. In all forty-plus of his years, this was perhaps second in revulsion to when he'd trailed to Pluto. The reason that held the top spot was that he'd been unable to affect anything then.

Now, he was only about ninety-five percent unable to affect the universe.

It seemed everything was happening *to* him, and he couldn't *happen* to anyone else.

First it had been Luna, who he'd refused to speak about with anyone since seeing the holovid a few days previously. He'd made up his mind what would happen there, and he didn't need input from his council or anyone else, for that matter. Those who had forced her into the marriage would die, and anyone who'd had a part in it—who had laid down a piece of carpet, who had set up a chair, who had poured a drink, anyone who had opened their *fucking* eyes at Luna would die. There wasn't anything he could do until he got to Earth, but death was coming for everyone involved.

Alistair had managed to force his attention to the task at hand, which was getting this massive force back to the planet Phoenix, then gearing up for the eight-planet warpath through the Commonwealth's territory.

"I'm beginning to not want to see you anymore, Thoreaux. All you do is bring me bad news."

Thoreaux had come with Servia. He held a DataTrack at his side, and both their faces were pale. They hadn't announced themselves or brought anyone else.

Alistair had just stepped out of the shower and still had a towel wrapped around his waist. They'd rung his quarters, and the looks on their faces had gained them entrance despite his state of undress.

"So no jokes, I'm taking it," Alistair said as he moved over to his bed. "What is it?"

Thoreaux spoke first. "The carrier we left to direct any stragglers or new people who decided to join our cause—do you remember it?"

Alistair nodded. "I did a walk-through before we left it, thanking the soldiers for remaining behind. Told them we'd save some killing for them when they caught back up."

Servia stepped to the small work table and quickly cleared the clutter off. "Just show him."

Thoreaux nodded, then placed the DataTrack on the table. He tapped the screen a few times, and a holovid came to life. He and Servia stepped back. "This came in about twenty minutes ago. Servia saw it and came to get me. It was highly encrypted, so most likely no one else has seen it, and it's best we keep it that way."

Alistair watched a recording from the carrier's point of

view. He was looking out into space and wouldn't have been able to see anything, but the holovid had highlighted the important objects in red.

Three of them.

"What is that?" he asked, staring at something that resembled an Earthborn squid with fewer tentacles. He saw the ship fire lasers and watched the squids dodge them.

"No clue," Thoreaux said.

Servia's face was fixed on the DataTrack. "Keep watching," she whispered.

Two corvettes launched from the carrier, highlighted in green on the backdrop of space's blackness.

Alistair blinked as he watched what happened to them. Two of the squids took them apart as if they were children's toys. The corvettes—machines built for the sole purpose of killing—were destroyed in mere minutes.

Alistair's eyes narrowed.

"I hate to say it," Servia chimed in, "but it gets worse."

Alistair knew what was coming, and he didn't want to watch it; all those souls who had chosen him were going to die. He didn't look away, though. He owed them that.

The squids hit the carrier like a hand hits a pool of water.

The holovid switched to cameras that tracked the squids as they pierced the vessel's armored walls. Their tentacles shredded and pummeled anything in their way. Nothing could withstand the punishment they dealt out. Fire ripped through hallways where oxygen still existed, burning men and women alive.

Thank the gods there weren't any children aboard, Alistair thought.

Finally, the holovid went black. There was nothing left to record the damage.

Alistair stood from his bed, staring at the spot the holovid had been. "What did I just see?"

"There's nothing like that in the universe, Pro," Thoreaux stated. "It doesn't exist."

Alistair turned his head to the ceiling. Water was still dripping down his body; he hadn't had time to dry off before they came in. "If they don't exist, those must be the AllSeer's. He's the only one with technology we don't understand. Has the AllMother seen it?"

"No," Thoreaux answered. "We brought it directly to you."

Alistair nodded and turned his back to them. "Let me finish getting dressed. Call the council, including the AllMother. They all need to see this. Leave the DataTrack. I want to watch it again."

"Got it," Thoreaux answered. He and Servia left the room quickly. Hopefully, everyone would be ready by the time he was.

"Jeeves," Alistair said to the room. "Can you reload that holovid?"

"Certainly."

Alistair hung the towel up and started putting on clothes.

"Rewind to the beginning," he told the AI, his eyes on the holovid as he threw a shirt on.

He watched the first twenty seconds. The ship had been

programmed to constantly record all the space around it. "Was it you or the captain that sent this, Jeeves?"

"As much as I'd like to take credit," the AI responded, "the captain gets it."

She must have known there was no hope, and her last act had been to get the word out. It had to have been quick, based on what Alistair had seen.

"Rewind it again."

The holovid went to the beginning while Alistair slipped on boots.

"Okay, Jeeves, load it in the war room. I'm heading there now."

"As you wish, sir," the AI said in its odd accent.

Alistair didn't bother looking at himself in the mirror. There wasn't time for vanity because what he'd just witnessed was worse than what Thoreaux and Servia probably thought.

He made his way to the war room, entering as others did. The AllMother was already sitting down, and she was the most important piece of this. Alistair didn't know how much help she'd be, but if anyone could understand this, it would be her.

"Everyone here?" Alistair asked as he did a quick mental check. Thoreaux, Servia, Relm, Faitrin, Caesar, and the AllMother.

"We're here," Thoreaux answered.

"Jeeves," Alistair told the AI, "show 'em."

The holovid came up again, and Alistair watched the whole thing. He felt the pang of guilt again when the squids hit the ship, but he shoved it down, compartmentalizing it. Right now, he had to keep his mind on the present and future. The past was lost to him.

When it was over, Relm was the first to speak. "They seem friendly enough."

The color had drained from everyone's faces except Caesar's and the AllMother's.

"Jeeves, play the first five seconds and put it on a loop," Alistair said.

They watched the beginning through a few times before Alistair made his point. "Whatever those things are, they're coming from the upper dimensions."

He watched the creatures appear to unfold as they entered the holovid's viewing range. Any time a ship, person, whatever, went up a dimension, it appeared as if they were folding in on themselves. When they went down, say, from fourth to third, they appeared to unfold.

That was what they were seeing here.

Alistair turned his attention to the AllMother. "Is it your brother?"

"Jeeves," she whispered, ignoring Alistair for the moment, "would you play it again?"

"Yes, madam," the AI responded. The holovid played through one more time. Alistair didn't watch but kept his eyes on the AllMother. She watched attentively, her eyes never leaving it. When it ended, the holovid didn't replay, and the room sat in silence, waiting for her to speak.

"Is it the AllSeer?" Alistair whispered.

Without looking at him, she gave a small nod. "It's Alexander. He's sent them after you."

Alistair crossed his arms over his chest. "What are they? Do you know?"

She shook her head, still staring at the empty place where the holovid had played. "No more than what you just saw."

"They're tracking me, you think?" he asked. "How? Why would they go to that ship?"

She met his eyes. "I don't know his powers anymore. His science. It's freakish to me, but there isn't any other explanation."

"Pro," Thoreaux said from the other side of the room. He was leaning against the wall. "You said you walked the ship, right?"

Alistair nodded, his eyes narrowing. "I've walked a lot of ships."

Thoreaux shrugged. "Might sound crazy, but maybe they're tracking your DNA? If they're traveling in the fifth dimension, that would be one reason they dropped down. They smelled your DNA, or whatever you want to call it."

"Can you even track DNA? Is that possible?" Alistair asked.

The AllMother tapped the table, letting the others know she wanted to speak. "I don't know about tracking DNA, but I know they're coming for you. I know my brother, regardless of how many years have passed. He wants you dead, and those...*things*...fit his *modus operandi*. They're overkill. They can destroy ships half the size of this dreadnought. Of course he would send them after you, Prometheus."

The conversation died as her words settled over everyone.

Relm broke the silence. "You got a plan for this one,

Pro? Or do you need me to come up with something? I've got a few minutes to spare."

Jeeves interrupted before Alistair could say anything. "My apologies, but I have another urgent message you are all going to want to see."

Relm groaned. Thoreaux straightened.

"Go ahead," Alistair instructed.

A holovid dropped from the ceiling. A Terram stood in the middle of the room, short and powerfully built. Alistair knew his face; he'd seen him before, which meant the Terram was of some importance, though Alistair didn't know his name. Thoreaux, Servia, and the AllMother dealt with the Terram for the most part.

The man spoke quickly in his native tongue, one Alistair still hadn't learned though it was he they followed.

He said nothing while the man's message came through. He watched his lieutenants' faces, trying to understand what they were hearing.

What he saw brought him no peace; whether it was the message alone or the combination of it and those squid creatures, he didn't know. He only knew what expressions their faces bore: sheer defeat.

Finally the message ended. Thoreaux swallowed once and looked at his leader. "The Commonwealth is going to attack Phoenix. They just dropped out of the fourth dimension, and they're hovering above the planet's atmosphere. They gave them an ultimatum: the Terram must give them the planet, or they're going to attack."

Alistair rubbed his hand through his hair, trying to get a handle on this new situation. "Is that just the overview, or is there anything else?"

"That's pretty much it, but Jeeves can give you a translation."

Alistair shook his head. "Give it to me later, Jeeves," he told the AI. He moved to the edge of the room and sat down in a chair, needing to think. His council slowly followed him over. Alistair bent forward, placing his elbows on his knees, and looked at the floor. He wasn't talking to them but himself.

"We've known the Commonwealth was still watching us, but our fleet's size must have told them what my plan was. Or someone leaked the information to a spy. Anything's possible, but it doesn't really matter now. They don't care about the Terram. They care about that portal."

He grew quiet for a second. No one else spoke. It might not have been fear in the room since they'd seen this man defy all odds so far, but something close to it permeated everything.

"It's a smart move. They're going to have the planet, and if we want the portal, we're going to have to take it from them. They want us to try, and then they plan on ending the insurrection before we ever make it back to the Milky Way."

He straightened, then leaned back in the chair and found Thoreaux's eyes.

His second in command tilted his head to the ceiling. "Jeeves, how far is the next nearest portal?"

The AI's voice filled the room. "I could give you a number, but it wouldn't matter. Even in the fourth dimension, it's prohibitively far. More, the Commonwealth could jump to that one if we headed that way. It's not a viable option, sir."

Thoreaux shook his head and looked at the floor. Servia spoke from his side. "What do you want to do?"

"I need to talk with Aspen, then I need some time to think. Keep on the current course."

"Do we send a message back to the Terram?" Servia asked.

"Tell them not to fight but to give up the planet. There's no need for them to die uselessly; the Commonwealth will get the planet if they want it. Plus, we'll need them for the battle." He paused for a second, then stood. "Tell them I'm on my way."

Aspen de Monaham never thought he'd get the position he now held. He'd also never wanted it.

He was now head of the Monaham family, but it was a job meant for someone else: his sister.

Cristin de Monaham.

The past few months had been the most tumultuous of Aspen's tumultuous life. His sister had been killed trying to expand her empire, and regardless of what had happened on that strange planet she'd gone to, the mantle of family leader had fallen on her younger brother—on Aspen.

He'd heard about those in his family shouting the man's name, screaming "*Ave*, Prometheus!" over and over when their fallen general had passed only moments before. It had made Aspen sick to his stomach to hear such things, and he'd sworn to kill every man, woman, and slave who had participated.

Aspen wasn't a cruel man by nature, but he'd loved his

sister, and he loved his family. It'd been a traitorous act to do such a thing.

It wasn't until the man that killed his sister showed up on Aspen's planet that his mind changed on that issue.

Aspen was five years younger than his sister, who had been a young leader. At nineteen, Aspen now owned a planet, and the man who'd killed the Ice Queen was upon it.

The Ice Queen's generals were being held captive, so only the elders were there to give him any advice. Attack the coming force or wait and hear what the man known as Prometheus had to say? Was he bringing fire to a planet made of ice?

The elders had told him to attack, but Aspen said he was going to wait. He was no warrior despite what his father had wanted from him.

The message that came from the dreadnoughts high above his planet was simple and shocking.

"My name is Alistair Kane, and I am the man who killed your queen. I am keeping your ships as spoils of war. I've returned to your planet for a few reasons, the first being to give you Cristin de Monaham's body so that you may perform whatever burial rites your culture practices. I've also brought anyone still living, and they can decide whether to stay with me or return to their homes.

"I'd also like to offer whoever leads this planet a choice. I have no quarrel with you and no wish to engage in battle. My war lies elsewhere. The option I'd like to give you is to join me. If you come, many will die, but I promise that if we win, your people will have more territory and power than they know what to do with. If you choose not to join me, you'll never see me again. In twenty-four standard hours, I will leave."

That was it. That had been the whole message.

The elders had told him to shoot at the ships and rain fire from the sky as they broke apart.

Aspen had invited the man who'd killed his sister down. He'd promised him safe passage and said he'd like to speak to him.

Aspen now understood that he'd remember their first conversation until the day he died.

If the gods existed, surely the man who entered his home was their progeny. He was tall, broad-shouldered like an ox, and each movement was so precise it looked calculated. Aspen understood why his sister had lost in hand-to-hand combat. Who could stand against such a creature?

They sat down across from each other at the dining room table. There was no one else in the room. Aspen had banished his guards. Prometheus' contingent remained in another room waiting.

"You said your war isn't here," Aspen began. "Where is it?"

"Another galaxy. The Milky Way."

"Who's it against?"

Prometheus' face didn't change when he said, "A man who tried to kill me."

Aspen leaned back in his seat. "All of that..." He pointed at the ceiling, toward where the fleet waited, "is for a man who tried to kill you?"

A little smirk grew on Prometheus' face. "It's a bit more complicated, but yes."

"You want my people to fight your war?"

"I respected your sister, even if she was cruel. Any people that can produce a leader like her is one I value. I don't expect you to come, but you should know that only about a third of those who fought on your side are planning to return. The rest are staying with me."

Aspen wasn't shocked. His sister had been the heart of this planet, just as his father had been before. Aspen would never be that beating heart. He understood his position was as a shepherd, and right now, regardless of what the elders thought, he knew how precarious it was. He couldn't protect this planet from invasion, especially not with so many leaving.

"Why don't you just enslave us?" Aspen asked.

Still smirking, the big man sighed. "I guess because I'm not a slave-driver. If you come, you'll still hold the position you're in. I don't know if you're a king or what, and I really don't care. You'll pledge fealty to me, and I'll protect your people like my own. When this is over, I guarantee your family won't be threatened for generations after you."

"No man can guarantee such a thing," Aspen said.

Prometheus leaned forward on the table. "I mean you no disrespect, but we both know your position. Your army is mostly mine. My intelligence says you're not like your sister or your brother. I didn't have to come here. I could have left the Ice Queen's body on the top of that roof and gone forward. I came because your family can help me, but I can also help them. It truly doesn't matter to me what you choose, but understand that you will lose this planet if you don't join. Other warlords will come here, and they *will* enslave you, those they don't kill. I'm giving you an out. A way to preserve your family and push your sister's legacy forward."

There had been more words and questions, but the choice had really come down to that. A stranger had understood and summed the problem up perfectly.

Aspen had pledged fealty, and the majority of his people had left the ice world over the next weeks. Some had refused, but there was nothing he could do about that.

Now, he and his family flew in dreadnoughts across the universe, heading toward a war Aspen didn't understand. He loved his family, his people, and he knew he wasn't the person to lead them, yet there was no one else.

He hadn't had much contact with Prometheus since they'd taken off, but the man now wanted to talk. The ship's AI had called ahead, alerting him that Prometheus would be docking within an hour.

Aspen met him in the docking bay. "*Salve*, Prometheus."

"*Salve*, Aspen," he responded formally. "Let's wait until we're in private to talk further."

They went to Aspen's quarters on the dreadnought, and when they were alone, Aspen asked, "You want a drink or anything? Food?"

Prometheus discarded the idea with a shake of his head. "How's Brillin working out for you?"

That had been Kane's only demand. He'd said Aspen had to take Brillin under his wing and teach him how to lead. The kid had fought for Pro against Cristin in that final battle, and he must have done well. Aspen wasn't stupid, though; he knew the boy was loyal to Prometheus and was probably keeping tabs on all that Aspen was doing. Making sure there wouldn't be an attempted coup.

"He's doing well," Aspen said. "It's clear he doesn't come from nobility, but he's got a good head on his shoulders. He's probably braver than I am." He was quiet for a moment. "I'm sure you didn't travel here to discuss him, though. What can I do for you, my liege?"

Prometheus sat down at the small dining table. "I hate that term. I'll never get used to it." He met Aspen's eyes. "We're going to war much faster than I thought we would, so we only have about two weeks to prepare. Can you get your family ready?"

Aspen was silent as he moved to the wet bar. He poured himself a strong drink and took a sip, his back to Prometheus. "You're not a dumb man. I'm not a warrior. I'm not a leader. I never wanted to be, but Cristin's need for expansion put me here." He turned around and met the former Titan's eyes. "I'm not the person you want in this position. You know why I joined. Because it was the smart move to keep those dependent on me alive. You don't have to keep me in this spot. I truly don't want it."

Kane was quiet for a moment, studying Aspen. Aspen didn't like it, didn't like the weight of this man's look. He understood why they called him Prometheus, bringing fire to humanity, but he thought Kane could just as easily burn the species to death with those flames. He was that strong —a world-breaker.

Alistair blinked, breaking the hold he held on Aspen, then leaned back in his chair and stared at the table. "I used to think a lot like you when I was a Titan. I always thought about the next mission. The next battle. In some ways, the position I'm in is a lot like the one you're in. I never wanted..." His eyes grew wide as he stared at the table. "I never wanted *any* of this, and while I always had choices about getting here, they weren't great ones. The choice was something like, lose your life or lead an insurrection. Here I am, though, and here you are. The problem with your thinking is you're only seeing the next battle, Aspen."

He looked up then. Aspen's eyes were narrowed; he was trying to understand what this man meant.

"There's going to be a lot of *next battles*, I imagine, but eventually, they'll end. Eventually, you're not going to be flying through space, doing my bidding. Eventually, your family is going to have their own planet again. Multiple ones, even. You're not a warrior, and maybe you'll never be one. What you need to consider, though, is this: are you the right person to lead during peace?"

Aspen didn't know how to respond. He found no words. He'd never considered the question just posed. He'd never considered any of this, and at nineteen years old, he didn't know the answer. He felt like he didn't know anything. His sister, now… She'd been different, groomed to take the mantle, but him?

"I don't know." It was the only answer he had.

Alistair stood from the table. "I believe you are that person, Aspen. You've got two weeks to get your men ready for battle. You don't need to be a warrior to be a leader. Your sister was smart, and unless you got fucked in the gene pool, I imagine you carry some of those brains too. Two weeks. Your liege commands it."

Alistair was alone as he flew back to his dreadnought in the corvette. The ship was running on auto-pilot, leaving Alistair the time he needed to think.

The price of leadership was loneliness; Alistair understood that as well as any person. The weight of entire civilizations rested on the decisions he was making, and the resources he had were limited while the forces against him grew more and more overwhelming.

Maybe he'd underestimated the Ascendant. Perhaps he'd always thought of the Commonwealth as a collective, strong because of all its people. Alistair now realized that had been a mistake. The driving force behind the collective was the Ascendant, and just because he'd never touched a battlefield, it didn't mean he wasn't a deadly foe. From a room on Earth, he was dictating the deaths of millions.

Alistair didn't know if Aspen could be the leader he needed. The head of the family was barely a man, and Alistair hadn't had time to understand him. Perhaps he should have made time, but it was too late for that now. He didn't have anyone he could give up to make sure Aspen's people were ready. All of his people would be needed for the already massive military he possessed.

Aspen would have to deliver.

What Alistair had told him wasn't a lie. It was what he believed the kid needed to hear.

The question now was, did he take over monitoring where Aspen was with his warriors, or did he delegate it?

Thoreaux *could* do it. There wasn't any doubt about his second's capabilities. Hell, any of his council could do it, but would it pull them away from their duties? Alistair understood better than everyone how bad this was going to be. Attacking a planet they didn't want to destroy and needing to save many of the people on it? The logistics alone were a nightmare, let alone the overarching strategy.

Luna's voice whispered in his head.

You brought the kid off his planet, Allie. You knew he was young. You knew he wasn't ready, and now you're tasking him with leading an army? It's your job to tutor him. It's your job to protect him until he's learned enough to protect himself. That's your job.

She was right. He couldn't pawn this off on anyone else.

Finally, as his corvette got close to the dreadnought, Alistair considered the actual issue.

Attacking the Commonwealth on a planet encased with fire, getting beneath the ground, then fighting in fortified tunnels. He was, for the moment, going to leave the squid creatures alone.

He had no choice in the matter. On a cold, calculating level, he couldn't complete this insurrection without the Terram. On a moral level, he had brought the Commonwealth to them, and he was as responsible for them as he was for the Monahams.

Alistair had to protect them, and if his movement was going to survive, he had to figure out a way to break free of the Commonwealth's paradigm. He had to do something they wouldn't expect.

Yet on a planet surrounded by flame, what bold move could he make to change things?

He had no ideas, yet his instructions to Thoreaux were the same: tell them help is on the way.

Was it a lie?

CHAPTER TEN

Two Months after Earth's Fleet Left for Phoenix

Petra stood next to the giant known as Hector and stared down at the planet called Phoenix. Their dreadnought was just above the atmosphere, where explosions continually detonated and flames always burned.

Petra had traveled next to the man for two months, racing through the fourth dimension for much longer than she'd ever traveled in it. When they'd finally reentered the third dimension, it was as if every part of her body sang in joy. Everyone she came in contact with appeared to feel the same, all having a spring in their steps.

Everyone except Hector. His body showed no joy, no change. If the fourth dimension affected him, Petra couldn't tell. Indeed, she could tell very little about the man. He'd been silent for much of the trip, offering no insights she could report to the Imperial Ascendant, though her leader hadn't called her either.

Petra's natural inclination to observe her surroundings was helping tremendously in this endeavor or would if

Hector would give her anything to work with. He didn't. The man was like a mountain, silent and unmoving, unbothered by the world around him.

Standing next to him, Petra was reminded of the mountain metaphor due to his size. She looked closer to a child than an adult when she was at his side, but for once, she wasn't concentrating on him.

Petra was staring at the world beneath their ship. The deck was a highly advanced panel, allowing the dreadnought to magnify whatever was outside it. Right now, it appeared as if they were only a few feet above the eternal flames.

"Have they given us word on whether they'll surrender or not?" she asked.

"It doesn't matter," Hector said without looking at her. He kept his eyes on the world beneath them.

Petra turned her attention to him. "What do you mean?"

"That was only a ploy to buy us time. Not all of our ships can travel at the same speed, and we want them all here before our attack. There's no reason for us to allow them quarter, especially not when their liege is on the way. It wouldn't do to give him a larger military when he does arrive."

She nodded. That made sense. It wasn't the most honorable thing they could do, but these Terram had pledged their loyalty to Kane after having remained neutral for so many years. This was war, and one side was going to have a lot of casualties. It was better that it be the Terram.

"The word will come down in a few hours. We launch

in ten standard, one hour before their deadline."

When Petra first began traveling with Hector, she'd been nervous about asking him questions. He had to know she was the Imperial Ascendant's plant, put there to spy on him. Yet, when she started asking questions, she felt no ill will from him. He was open and honest with his answers, and when he couldn't tell her for whatever reason, he didn't shy away from it. He didn't treat her like an equal—Hector was obviously her superior—but he didn't treat her like an inferior either. They were comrades; that was the closest name she could find for it.

Petra had to remember her purpose here; a strong leader or someone who was kind to her could still over-throw the Commonwealth. They could still cast everything she knew and loved back into the Dark Ages. Her purpose here hadn't changed, nor would it.

"Have you fought in something like this before?" Hector asked.

It was only the two of them in this small room. The rest of the dreadnought was abuzz with action, but here, there was peace.

"No," Petra answered with a shake of her head. "I've had a few assignments on Earth, but it wasn't warfare like this. The Academy staged some war-like exercises, but...no. Nothing like this."

He nodded as if he'd known the answer. "A lot of people are going to die when we start this, on both sides. This planet is better fortified than any I've ever seen, and the atmosphere creates even more difficulty. We'll be fighting under the ground inside tunnels that are built for them, not us." He was calm as he spoke, showing no anxiety or anger. "Stay close to me, Petra. I'm not saying you're not skilled or that your Titans aren't, but this is very different from the assignments you usually take on."

He paused for a moment.

"I'll keep you alive, Petra, but you have to stay close. Understand?"

"What about everyone else?"

Hector glanced at her from the corner of his eye, and a smirk appeared on his lips. "The Ascendant didn't send them to spy on me. They're on their own."

Petra wore her MechSuit as she strapped herself into the Digger. It was a deep green, like a plant from a lush jungle. Her Whip was attached to her belt, as well as the various other weapons she would use.

Across the fleet, others were doing the same. They couldn't just collapse the interior of the planet, crushing the Terram in their tunnels; that would also break their portal. Destroying that would cause Kane to seek other means of returning to the Commonwealth. No, it would be hand-to-hand combat for the most part. They'd take the planet inch by bloody inch.

The Digger was new for Petra, though Hector had explained it to her briefly before they started launch prep. He'd used a smaller version on Mars when the Subversives had dug themselves into the planet.

The machine could withstand the heat, including almost anything except a direct explosion. It would latch onto the planet, then use scanning tech to map the area beneath it before drilling in such a way that it wouldn't collapse the surrounding area. It would allow the tunnels to remain structurally intact. Petra didn't know how any of that was possible, especially with the tremendous heat above them, but Hector said it would work.

It'd better, given the number of Diggers that would be launched toward the planet. If it didn't? It'd be a lot of dead Commonwealth soldiers since this was the first stage of their assault. Some of the smaller ships would enter the atmosphere and begin subterranean scans, mapping the Terram world. Once that was finished, the Diggers would basically form tunnels to the transports and bring more men. The side facing space would open, creating an airlocked tunnel that would connect to the transports flying in from space.

That was yet another tactic Petra hadn't heard of, but Hector said it too would work.

The Digger was a massive circular ship that looked like a saucer rather than a typical transport. Petra sat next to Hector, her helmet retracted into the neckline of her suit for the time being. She'd already taken in the area around her. The seats were in circular rows, becoming larger as they got closer to the outer edge of the ship.

This Digger contained five hundred people, and some were smaller, some were larger. It depended on the size of the underground tunnel the human payload was being dropped at.

Hector was strapped in next to Petra. She'd heard of his dual sabers, and she saw the black handles strapped across his massive back. The two of them were in the front row, and he was staring forward while not appearing to look at anyone.

Her Titans were to her left and behind her, as well as the Martians, though their armor was closer to the Titans' than Hector's. It was a dull red like the world they stemmed from, and the faceplate covered their entire face. The heads-up display or HUD was inside their helmet instead of outside like Petra's, and the large faceplate gave them more real estate for it.

Petra put the Martian-to-Titan ratio at seventy-thirty, which made sense. Hector would want to surround himself with his own army for battles.

A new and strange thought came to her. *Does he think one of us might try to kill him? Does he think I might try to kill him?*

She glanced at the large man next to her. If he feared anything, none of it showed. His helmet sat between his feet, and his face showed only calm. No anger, no fear, no bloodlust.

He'd told her, *"I'll keep you alive, Petra, but you have to stay close"* as if she were a child who needed his help, yet he hadn't said it to mock her, and at the time, she hadn't taken offense. Only looking back now did she see where she could have grown angry at such a slight.

Petra was a Titan. She didn't need help or support from anyone.

If she'd told Hector that, he would have simply nodded, exhibiting this same calm, and she would have felt even more childlike.

"Digger One ready to launch in ten…nine…eight…"

Hector bent down and picked up his primitive helmet, then placed it on his lap. It had no HUD in or outside it.

"Seven...six...five..."

Petra pulled up her helmet and turned her own HUD on.

"Four...three...two..."

The bottom of the ship suddenly grew transparent, and Petra found herself staring down at flames. The dreadnought's dock had opened for them. The ship lunged down, and the flames appeared to engulf Petra. Her HUD's display showed that the internal temperature wasn't rising, but she shuddered as they plunged through the fiery atmosphere. She couldn't see to the bottom of the fire, the orange and yellow too thick for her to view the planet's surface.

Lasers broke through the bright mask of color. The Terram were obviously able to see them as they rushed downward. The ship rocked to the right, then back to the left, the AI trying its best to avoid the ground attacks and aerial explosions.

Petra looked at Hector.

He was still staring forward. His face hadn't changed expression.

Petra turned her attention to the floor again.

A laser burst through the flames and hit the outside of the ship about five meters from where she sat. Petra rocked to the left, her body straining against the seat's restraints. The laser spread across the floor, the armor outside holding. She didn't know how long it would continue to do so, though, not after the jolt she'd felt.

Hector still showed no emotion. No surprise.

The AI's voice came over her helmet's comm. "Digger One impact in seven seconds."

The cloud of flames disappeared, and Petra was staring at burned sand. There was another jolt as the ship's legs, which had unfolded from the sides, dug into the ground beneath it. The floor turned opaque again, and the ship vibrated as the mighty drill began its work. Now was the most vulnerable time for everyone inside the Digger. There was nowhere to move, no way to dodge an attack. They could only wait for the machine to finish what it was made to do.

Minutes passed in silence, each one feeling like an eternity to Petra. Adrenaline coursed through her veins. She wanted out of this container. She was ready to do what she'd been trained for, yet when she stole another glance at Hector, she saw none of those emotions in him. He didn't seem to realize where he was or what was going on around him. It was as if he were watching a movie that only he could see, one that evoked calm in the viewer.

The AI spoke again, the only sound besides the ship's machinations. "Unloading in ten seconds. Prepare for battle."

Hector took his helmet off his lap and placed it on his head. He reached over his shoulders with both hands and grabbed the sabers' hilts. His massive hands held them firmly in his lap.

Petra took her Whip off her belt as the opaque floor beneath her began folding in on itself.

Hot air rushed into the ship from below, the earth almost as hot as the outside from the drill's work. Petra's HUD told her the drop would be about twenty meters, and her chair straightened and tilted so that she was straight and her feet were facing the tunnel.

The straps unlatched and she fell. She kept her Whip furled; opening it now would surely slice open one of the people dropping next to her.

Within seconds, she hit the ground. Her suit absorbed the impact and her Whip unfurled, ready to defend and attack. She quickly scanned her surroundings, finding that they weren't in a tunnel but some sort of arena. Petra looked back at the ceiling, and she saw that the Digger was still locked in, keeping the dangerous flames outside from whipping in and waiting for more soldiers to arrive and drop through the tunnel it had created.

All of those observations took mere seconds, then she heard the first attack.

She turned to the right, looking like a metal warrior inside her armor. The stands in this arena were lined with soldiers, squat-looking humans who held rifles.

Not even a moment later, she heard Hector in her comm. "Stay close to me, Bird. They mean to shoot you down from the sky."

He'd never called her such a thing before, but there wasn't time to consider it. The calm was gone from his voice, and when Petra looked up, she couldn't have mistaken him for anyone else.

Hector was bounding through the crowd of soldiers. Anyone in his way dropped to the ground as he rushed past them. Petra took off after him, following the tunnel he'd created through the enemy.

He was about five meters in front of her when he did something she wouldn't have thought possible; he slammed a massive foot on the ground and launched himself into the air. He was going to clear the stands surrounding the arena without any MechGear to support him. Petra almost paused in awe at the feat, but adrenaline kept her pushing onward.

Seconds after he'd landed in the stands, she leapt about two meters in front of where he'd jumped, not confident she could make that leap even with the suit helping.

Petra landed and her Whip went to work. She sliced through the first two Terram she saw. Their backs were to her as they aimed their weapons at the terror sweeping through them. Petra glanced up to watch Hector, once again feeling the urge to stop what she was doing and watch this creature. For the first time, she thought he might not be human or mutant, but something altogether different—a *new* creature. Lasers shot at him, sabers tried to bring him down, yet he kept moving. His muscles were visible, almost unaided by armor, and his sabers cut through people as if they were plants on a farm.

She watched as he lifted one of the sabers to his shoulder, the back half of the laser pointing behind him. It shot out like a bullet, striking the chest of an enemy Petra had hardly noticed.

The saber's laser recharged, and he kept moving across the stands.

Petra heard him again. "Come on, Bird. You're falling behind. Don't let all this glory be mine."

Inside her helmet, she couldn't help but smile. Other Martians and Titans were clearing the stands now, and Petra had no idea what Hector was telling them in their comms. For all she knew, he could be telling them to cut her down, yet she didn't think that was so.

The Terram were falling, and Petra bounded toward Hector, moving past the dead and dying. She caught up, and together they killed more of the traitors, more of those who had sold out the Commonwealth for the first flash of gold they saw.

Together, they took the stands, clearing the way for the soldiers who would come after. When they reached the end, Hector turned to look at the Martians and Titans. Some lay dead, but the vast majority stood staring at him.

Petra was next to him, but she knew no one in the stands or below on the arena floor saw her. They were looking at the majestic warrior who'd led them into battle.

"*Ave*, Hector!" nearly everyone shouted, caught up in their clear victory.

Petra said no such thing and was shocked at Titans giving such praise to this man. Anger mixed with her bloodlust and she turned her head slightly to the right, looking at the helmeted beast.

"It's okay, Bird," he said through her comm. "Don't be too angry at them. They still love the Commonwealth; they're just overwhelmed right now. Come, there's more to do and no time to rest on one win."

If Petra could see everything in a room at nearly the moment she walked in, this man could tell the emotions of a person with almost the same speed.

Hector hopped down from the stands, leading his army into the halls of death.

There was no final battle, no great fight between two stone-cold killers. The Terram fought as hard as they could, battling in the small tunnels they'd built, using hidden weapons to kill Martians and Earthborn alike. The Commonwealth simply kept coming. They threw more and more soldiers into the tunnels, what seemed like endless numbers of them. The scanning technology allowed them to send reinforcements where necessary, and so few Diggers were shot down that a steady supply of warriors continued streaming out of the dreadnoughts above.

Petra followed Hector through the tunnels, killing where there was room for her to do so but mostly watching the huge man mow down all comers. He'd taken a few wounds on his uncovered arms and legs, but he appeared to not feel them. As his backup, Petra thought he might be a machine and wondered if she were to cut into him, would she find metal pieces where bone should be?

For hours they fought, going deeper into the planet as the Terram fought and died, retreating farther into their home.

Finally, the word came from Petra's Primus. "No more advancing. We rest and heal for the next six hours. Martian and Earthborn unit leaders should be prepared for more messages to come."

Petra felt the adrenaline leave her system. Her body suddenly grew weak, and it was a struggle to remain standing. Her HUD showed they'd been fighting for almost five hours, clearing tunnel after tunnel.

She looked behind her. There were a lot fewer soldiers than there had been in the arena. Many had fallen as

Hector advanced. Terram lay dead throughout the tunnels, and weapons were scattered over the ground, both rifles ripped from the walls and pistols that had fallen from now-cold hands.

Hector turned to look at the men and women who'd followed him for the past few hours. There was no one left to kill in this tunnel. They would have had to continue deeper into the planet to find more of the enemy. Hector sheathed his sabers on his back, then removed his helmet and held it against his side. Blood covered the metal helmet, and Petra saw that it covered his face as well. She could only imagine what her own suit looked like—a bloody massacre.

"Today, you've all proven your worth to the Commonwealth. Go, rest and heal. There's much fighting left to do."

Petra heard no *Ave, Hector* this time, and she was glad for it. The warriors were tired, and they weren't concerned with anything but finding a place to rest their heads or a meal to shovel into their mouths before the next battle came. She understood that since she felt the same. This had been no Subversive battle. The Terram had been well-armed and fought hard but were simply overwhelmed.

The tunnel cleared out, but Hector didn't move, and neither did Petra. She could still hear the battle raging nearby, or at least feel the vibrations. The war hadn't stopped because the announcement came, but over the next hour or so, silence would take the place of the violence.

Hector squatted, placing his helmet in front of him. He turned it over so he could peer inside, then touched two fingers to the spot closest to the spine. The helmet began to slide into itself. Hector didn't look up as it shrank. "You fought well today, Bird. Only a few men have seen this happen with my helmet, and I'm not sure if you've earned it, but I'm too damned tired to carry the thing back at full size."

Petra let her own helmet retract into her neckline. "Why do you keep calling me that? Bird?"

He shrugged as his helmet finished shrinking. It was now about the size of his massive palm and twice as thick. He picked it up and placed it on his belt. From his squatting position, he looked up at her. "You looked bird-like when we fell out of the Digger. The rest of us fell like anvils, but you seemed to fly."

He stood up then. "You don't have long to rest. I don't know what reports you have to give, but I expect you to be in the same shape you are now in a few hours. The fighting isn't going to get easier."

Petra followed him as he walked. "I'll be fine. Will you? Did you save anything else? You fight with total abandon. You've got to be exhausted, too."

"No, it only appears that way. I give what the situation calls for, no more. I'll be fine."

"What are you going to do now?" she asked as they turned down the tunnel to a stairwell. The door had been blown off its hinges and was lying on top of a dead soldier. He looked to be a Terram, but his head was gone, so Petra couldn't be sure.

"I have my own reports to give. Meetings. Strategy. On my planet, I made the strategy, but here I take it from your Primus and others. I'll need to put their ideas into tactics we can use for the next battle."

"Do you want me with you?" Petra asked.

He shook his head. "No, you need to rest and get ready for the next part, Bird. The deeper the Terram go, the bloodier it's going to get."

Hector allowed himself a quick shower and dressed, then sent the briefest message back to Luna, basically letting her know he was alive. Hector knew the Ascendant understood the game his grandfather had launched, but he was going to keep playing his part. He was a husband now, so he would need to keep in touch with his wife as things progressed.

Appearances had to be kept up.

Hector hadn't been lying to Petra about what would come next. These Terram fought like madmen.

No, he told himself. *They fought like men and women about to lose their homes.*

Which they were, every one of them.

None of the warriors now inside the planet had headed back to the ships. It would waste too much time, and if too many left, it could allow the Terram to create strongholds in areas that had already been taken. The Terram could probably cause the world to cave in on itself, but the risk to them was too large. Their liege needed the portal near the core as well, and they wouldn't chance destroying that.

No, it was safe and expedient to use the tunnels and rooms the Commonwealth had taken.

Hector checked his DataTrack, found where the meetings would be held, and made his way through the bloody tunnels. The lower class of military was pulling the dead out of them. They'd all be incinerated in the atmosphere above, friend and foe alike.

The tunnels were small for the big man, and he found himself ducking much of the time. It'd been hard to battle in such small spaces, and he hadn't been capable of using his physicality to its maximum. So far, he hadn't needed to, but he wasn't built for fighting in spaces like this.

He found the room where the Primus was holding his first meeting. Hector hadn't met him except in meetings like this, but he seemed like a fair enough man. His name was Jovan de Washten, though those close to him called him Jove. Hector knew the basics about him, primarily because he needed to know all of those close to the Ascendant. The man was in his late thirties, was still in great physical shape, and had been third in line to his newly minted position. Most likely, he would never have made it so high, but with Kane's, then Ares' dismissal, he'd been promoted.

Hector respected the man and wondered what would happen when it came time for him to choose Caius or Alexander.

Hector took a seat in the back of a room that had been carved from hard rock. He listened and kept his eyes on the Primus as he listed the successes and failures but found his mind going back to Petra.

Hector knew why she was here; the Ascendant hadn't been subtle about it. He realized he liked the young woman, but more than that, he respected her. It was a different kind of respect than what he felt for Luna. That was a survivor's respect, born from a refusal to let outside forces fully determine her life. Petra wasn't like that.

Hector had never let anyone close to him. There'd been no second in command for him on Mars. Each mission had different parameters, different experts, different people he had to learn to work with. All of it had been for a reason, of course—to refine his military leadership capabilities.

He'd watched Petra today, though, and he had been struck by her ferocity, but more, by her intelligence. Someone that size, regardless of the MechSuit she wore, would never be able to use brute force to win a battle. She hadn't even tried that, and Hector had not had to save her very often. She used her body the way it was made to be used, and she assisted it with an able and quick mind.

Hector had seen every moment she could have attempted to slide her Whip into his back, but he was fairly confident she hadn't considered it. Perhaps those weren't the Ascendant's orders, though maybe they had been. Either way, she'd fought by his side honorably.

Hector would keep her alive through this, though he now knew he wouldn't have to carry her. She'd hold her own. The question was the same for her as it was for this Primus: which side would she join when the final decision had to be made?

At the mention of Kane, Hector's mind focused on de Washten.

"Kane's forces will be here in nine days. That's our focus." The Primus eyed each of his lieutenants. "We've got three days to complete the sack of Phoenix, then another six days to prepare for his attack. I guarantee you, good sirs and ladies, *his* will be much more dangerous."

CHAPTER ELEVEN

Veena's experience on the machine world had been similar to Ares'. However, she'd not known anything of the sort was taking place with him until after her own digital world fell apart in flakes, leaving her in darkness.

When she woke, she'd found herself lying next to Ares about two kilometers from their ship. There'd been no machines around her, and she hadn't moved for quite some time. Veena didn't know if Ares was alive or dead, and at that moment, she hadn't cared.

In the final room she'd ventured into, her mother and father had been waiting for her. She'd known it wasn't them, but she'd wondered why the intelligence had used her parents? What was the point of that?

Much of her life, if not the majority of it, had been spent trying to shove them away because to recognize that loss would have been too much. It would have derailed her life, making Primus only an unrealized dream.

Yet as she lay on the hard red rock, Primus *was* only a

dream. One from the past, and not something she'd ever see again.

It wasn't until Ares moved slightly that she snapped out of her thoughts. So much more had happened on this planet, more than she could fathom. It was only the strength—and perhaps the neglect—of her feelings regarding her parents that had kept her from considering the rest.

She turned her head to the right and looked at her partner. He was in his MechSuit, the helmet retracted. "You alive?"

He was staring at the sky. He blinked once. "I think so. Do you feel it?"

It took Veena a moment to realize what he was talking about, but once she did, she couldn't *not* feel it.

"They encoded it in us," Ares whispered. "Half in me, half in you. It's encrypted, but it's there."

"How's that possible?" she asked. "I can...*feel* it, but I can't read it. I can tell there's coding, something new." The closest thing she could compare it to was some kind of growth on her body, perhaps a new mole. It didn't belong on her, but she couldn't deny its existence, even if she didn't understand it.

"It's time to go."

Veena almost groaned at the sound of the voice. It was the godsawful machine that had delivered her meals, or what she had thought were meals. It'd all been a digital creation, except apparently this machine was real.

Ares tilted his head up. "Monk, what in hades are you doing here?"

Veena sat up, not understanding the name but not caring at the moment.

The machine rolled over the rocks, stopping about a meter from them. "My home is no more. My purpose is with you two now, to ensure you don't fuck up what's been given to you."

"What?" Veena turned to look in the direction where the machine city had been. "Oh, my gods!"

It was gone. All the buildings, contraptions, *machines*—there was nothing left. No smoking ruins, no empty streets. There was just...nothing.

Ares was on his feet in a few seconds. "How is that possible? How is *any* of this possible?"

Monk rolled up to Ares as Veena climbed to her feet. "Our purpose was to find you two. Now that we've found you, our purpose has changed. None of what we were is necessary anymore. All that is necessary is me, so the rest could be destroyed."

Veena's eyes narrowed as she stared at the empty space. "Are you the keeper? The one I met?"

"A version, yes," the machine answered, "but in many ways, no. That isn't important right now. We are unprotected on this planet, and it's time to go."

Veena was still trying to grasp what lay in front of her—or rather, what *didn't* lay in front of her. Where had it all gone? The problem was, she didn't know how long she'd been out. She didn't even know the year, let alone the day.

Ares whirled on the machine, obviously angry about what had just occurred. "What do you mean, unprotected? This planet is so far beyond any known worlds, there's no one who can possibly hurt us."

The machine cocked its head sideways, looking oddly like an Earth praying mantis to Veena's eyes. "Why we gave the algorithm to you, I shall guess my entire life. Are you so stupid as to not remember the creatures you were kept with? Even if they were a digital representation, you should have been able to see how many tried to reach this world."

Ares shook his head. "Nah, that's bullshit. The way station we went through said hardly anyone had passed through it before us. Whatever we saw in there, you made us see."

The machine turned to look at Veena, who was still staring at the vanished city. "I trust you are not as obtuse as this one?"

Veena decided there wasn't anything else to stare at. Whatever had been was no more. She turned to the machine—Monk, as Ares had called it. "I like to think I'm less obtuse, but what he says is true. So either it's lying to us, you're lying to us, or there are other paths to this planet."

"Definitely not as obtuse," Monk responded. "There are many paths to this planet, and given how long it's existed, many have tried to take them. Some for the algorithm, some for the tech, some for reasons I can't begin to understand, but regardless, eyes watch this planet. The Commonwealth isn't the only powerful entity in this universe, nor are humans the only species, despite how highly you think of yourselves."

Veena understood at the same time Ares did. She tilted her head to the sky. "So, if they're looking now, they're going to see very soon that the planet is uninhabited?"

"'Very soon' is a relative term, and it also depends on where the scouts are. The point is that we are not safe, and every moment we remain here, we grow less safe." Monk turned his head toward Ares. "Do you understand now?"

The former Titan's hand went to his Whip. The machines had given it back, just like his suit. "Careful, Monk. We came a long way without you. It won't take much to do it again."

Again the machine looked at Veena. "Is he always so sensitive?"

"You get used to it." Veena didn't care about their bickering. She understood the danger they were facing, and she wanted to get out of here. On her ship, she'd be better able to deal with any threats. Here, she was basically defenseless. She started walking toward the ship, not looking behind her to see if the others were coming.

She heard Ares speak as she walked.

"You must have gained a sense of humor when you tore your city down, Monk, because you weren't this fuckin' jovial when you held me captive."

Veena heard Monk's treads roll over the rocky ground. "I've turned my humor gauge up to deal with you."

"Well, turn it down," Ares said.

"Fortunately, my makers didn't give control over that to you," the machine responded.

"You couldn't have given us a better ship?" Ares asked Monk once they'd escaped the planet's atmosphere. "All that tech, and you left us with this?"

"What you come with is what you leave with. What we gave you is possibly worth more than all the ships in the universe, combined." Monk was staring at one of the ship's panels, looking out at space. Ares imagined it was the first time the creature had ever been off his home planet. He was giving the machine a hard time, but in reality, he didn't hold any ill will toward it.

"I'm not seeing any enemies coming for us, Monk. You sure you aren't just a bit paranoid?"

The machine didn't turn to look at him as he spoke. "They're coming. We weren't fast enough. They're already flocking to the planet, and soon they'll be on us as well."

Ares didn't like the sound of that. He turned to Veena with an eyebrow raised.

She only shrugged and shook her head, saying nothing. She continued to watch her scans.

"So far I'm right, Monk, but I'll play along. Do they know we have the algorithm?" Ares still found it hard to believe that such a thing was in his mind, yet any time he doubted it, he had only to close his eyes and feel it.

"I wasn't programmed with the ability to read minds," the robot shot back.

"You know what I mean. Why are they coming for us? That doesn't make sense, given the myth."

Monk still didn't look at him but peered at the starlit panel as if he could see the coming enemies. "Just because the algorithm didn't spread, it doesn't mean the rumor of it didn't. Rumors spread like the wind, and people spread at nearly the same pace. An algorithm such as the one you came looking for would be a valuable rumor and would probably spread even faster."

Ares again turned to Veena, but she was staring at the panels as well, her eyes glazed as if she weren't hearing them. Ares was trying to get the logic of their situation laid out so he could understand it since if Monk was right, there wouldn't be much time for understanding later.

Veena's question had little to do with the logic behind everything, though, or at least the logic that didn't directly concern her.

"Why did I see my parents?" Her eyes kept that glazed look. "What was the point of that?"

Monk turned then, his human-like head the only part of his body that moved. "We had to understand you. The human species is more defined by their parental units than any other species we've come across. Your entire lives are molded by what your parents do and say, sometimes to greatness and other times to sorrow. Oftentimes, the two are combined."

"Why did I see them, then?"

Ares couldn't tell if there were tears in Veena's eyes, but he thought maybe there were. He hadn't seen her cry ever, not in all they'd experienced together, yet now...

Monk rolled back from the screen a bit, then straightened so he faced the ship's captain. "Humans use different coping mechanisms to deal with their lives. We do not judge those mechanisms, but we needed to understand them to decide who would receive the cargo you now carry. That was our part in this. It is mostly finished, besides me. Your part is just beginning, and like we needed to understand your coping mechanisms, you must as well. To accomplish what is necessary, you'll have to face the things you've shoved down, Veena de Ragnimus."

The machine was quiet for a moment, and Ares dared not interrupt that silence. The tears in Veena's eyes were undeniable now, and Ares was not so dense as to let his arrogance shine through.

When Monk spoke, his voice held no bedside manner, no deference. "If you don't deal with them, you'll die during what is to come."

The AI had taken over flight duties, along with Monk, though the machine showed no interest in anything about the ship. All he—*it*—seemed concerned with was staring into the screens for invisible enemies.

Veena had gone to her cabin to try to sleep, unsure if it would come.

Showing that emotion in front of Ares, let alone the machine, hadn't been something she wanted to do, but she'd needed to know.

What did her parents have to do with any of this?

Now she knew, or at least she knew what the machine had told her.

She was lying on her back atop the covers, clothes still on, when Ares' face showed on the panel to the right of her door.

"Let him in," she whispered to the AI.

The door slid open, but Ares didn't step inside. "You mind if we talk for a few minutes?"

"As long as we don't talk about my parents, I don't care."

"That's fine by me." He stepped into the room, and the door slid shut behind him. "You've checked the ship's systems, right? Security protocols? All that stuff I know nothing about?"

"I've run the checks three times since we boarded," she answered. "If the machines did anything to the ship, there's no trace of it. There's no evidence of an AI memory wipe, either. Everything is as it was."

Ares remained standing and started to pace in the small room, going from one wall to the other. "This isn't making any sense to me, Veena. We should dump the machine into space right now and rethink where we're heading."

Currently, they were in the fourth dimension and heading back to the last waystation they'd encountered. Monk said it no longer existed either, and Veena believed him. Veena hadn't had time to consider where they'd go from there.

"What would you rather we do?" she asked, sounding weary. "We've got the algorithm, but we didn't think about what we were going to do once we got it. I don't think we can sell it in its current form."

Ares had to know she was right about that. Whatever was inside their heads…whatever had been *inserted* in them was encrypted. If she was still using the mole analogy, the mole's skin was covered in titanium, and there was no way to get inside it.

"I'm not sure what we can do with it, actually," she continued. "From what the machine makes it sound like, about the only thing we can do is run since other people are going to want it."

"That's what I'm not understanding," Ares responded. He reached one end of the room and turned around, but he didn't move forward. He looked at her on the cot. "These machines, put there by the gods only know who, gave *us* the algorithm, but clearly not for monetary gain. They've protected it for a thousand years, maybe more, yet they gave it to *us*, people who abandoned their posts and maybe their final mission. Now, you and I are just going to believe that? We're just going to go along with it, letting this machine aboard our ship when it could self-destruct at any point and leave us floating through space, most likely in pieces."

Veena closed her eyes. She was exhausted, and she thought once she finally slept, she'd see her parents again. "Just tell me what you want me to do, Ares. If you want to dump the machine, we can do it when I wake up. Or hades, you can do it now. I honestly don't care. I just want to sleep."

She heard Ares pacing again, his energy uncontainable. He had to burn it off somehow, apparently. "I know what I want to do, and I don't care what the machine wants. I haven't decided whether he's a help or a hindrance. It doesn't really matter *why* that planet was there, either, not with what I want."

He'd reached the other side of the room and stopped, but he didn't turn this time.

"What *do* you want?" Veena asked.

"I want to go back to Earth, and I want to take down whatever artificial intelligence the Ascendancy uses. That's why the person stole it to begin with, isn't it?"

Veena opened her eyes. "We'll die. I doubt we'd even make it back into the Solar System. Spies, bounty hunters, the fucking people the machine says are hunting us... someone will get us."

Ares still didn't turn around. "If you can figure out how to sell the code in our heads, I'm all for it. Otherwise, we're going to be running forever. All we've done since we left Earth was escape death. I'm fine to keep escaping it."

What could Veena say, no? If that planet had folded up, all the machines simply disappearing... They'd entrusted this algorithm to the two of them, and Veena was positive it wasn't to sell it to the highest bidder. "If I go along with you, will you let me sleep?"

Ares faced her, and she could hear the arrogant smile in his voice. "Of course. If you do what I want, I'll quit bothering you."

"Fine. Let's go get caught by the people who are chasing us. What do you want to do with the machine?"

"You don't have a preference?"

"Just to rest. That's all I want."

The grin disappeared. "I'll take care of him."

Ares' Whip was attached to his belt, and his hand touched the top of the hilt as he entered the bridge.

The machine was in the same place it had been, still staring out at the blackness of space.

Ares wasn't sure what the thing was capable of, but he didn't trust it. A digital representation of the thing had been his captor for what felt like weeks. After leaving Veena to sleep, Ares had checked the scans the ship had run on it when it entered. There didn't appear to be any self-detonating equipment inside it, though the scan identified weapons.

Ares remained at the bridge's entrance, his hand still on the Whip's hilt. "We've decided where we're going, Monk."

The machine didn't turn around. "And where's that?"

"We're going back to Earth. We're going to deliver this algorithm back to the source and shut down the AI created from it." He took a step onto the bridge, removing his Whip from his belt. "I want to know what your purpose here is, Monk. No more bullshit. No more games."

The machine didn't turn around to look at Ares. It didn't move at all. "My purpose is to make sure you return to Earth and implant the algorithm into the intelligence residing there. That is my entire reason for existing, and after that, I'm unsure of what will happen to me."

Monk turned around so the two were looking at each other.

"We wouldn't have given you the algorithm if we thought there was any real chance that the algorithm wouldn't have been returned to its source."

Ares stared at the creature, wishing it showed some semblance of humanity—something he could read. "You support us going there? I won't have to watch my back the entire time, wondering if you're going to try to kill me? Or Veena?"

"If we wanted you dead, Romulus, don't you think you'd already be dead? We've gone into your head, into your dreams, and given the time we have left, you're the best chance we have of completing this, you and Veena."

Ares took his hand off the Whip. "Where did you come from, Monk?"

"My maker didn't gift me with that information, as your species' maker didn't either. Perhaps they're the same, or perhaps one modeled itself after the other. I don't know, and it's not my purpose to know. It isn't your purpose any longer either. Your purpose is the same as mine now: returning to the source with the gift you've been given."

"I'm trusting you, Monk, and it's not something I'm doing lightly. I care about Veena, and for some reason, I still care about Earth." Ares paused for a second, not sure how to say what he wanted. "I guess I hope you're telling the truth."

"I am, Romulus," Monk said. He turned around again and faced the screens. "Go sleep. I will stand watch. You're going to need your rest."

CHAPTER TWELVE

The AllSeer was resting when word came to him. The message came into the capsule he lay inside, and the irony wasn't lost on him. It was the capsule he'd woken from, and now it was the one he rested in.

The algorithm is moving.

The message was simple, and the AllSeer had been waiting to hear it for hundreds of years.

The capsule opened, and he swung his legs to the side and stepped to the floor.

"Show me," he said to the slave waiting for him.

The slave cast a holovid from the ceiling, showing the AllSeer the planet he'd been watching for so long. It looked as he remembered it, all metal and machine-like—impenetrable even for him. He had tried breaking through their defenses time and again, but each time, his forces had fallen. He'd done everything but show up there and had finally decided to simply watch the planet. Fate was on his side, so he waited.

"It took about twenty-four standard hours for the image to reach us," the slave said.

The AllSeer watched, his calm demeanor slowly turning to amazement. In a lifetime that had seen almost everything imaginable, this was something new.

Everything constructed on the world began to fold in on itself. The AllSeer's view was magnified, giving him a closer look than would otherwise have been possible. He watched as skyscrapers collapsed in a controlled manner, panel after panel folding into the one beneath it.

He could even see the largest machines shrinking, the entire planet disappearing one metal part at a time.

The machines and buildings broke apart, and the AllSeer watched huge swarms of bee-like steel rush through the air, heading to the machine capital. When they arrived, they didn't slow but slammed into the collapsing buildings to meld with that metal.

The AllSeer witnessed an entire civilization fall into itself. He said nothing, only now beginning to understand what was happening—or had already happened.

At the end of the collapse, two machines remained on the world. One was a ship, another a droid.

The ship took off with the droid and two humans on it.

"Our closest ship can meet theirs in three standard days, master," the slave told him.

The algorithm was loose in the universe once again. The AllSeer had missed the first opportunity to take it, and despite his best efforts, been thwarted repeatedly by the machine world.

If there had ever been a better example of the AllSeer's belief in fate, he could not find it. The entire universe was coalescing around his homecoming.

"Connect with the ship's commander," he told the slave.

A few moments passed, then a voice filled the room.

"Master, this is Victor. How may I serve you?"

"You have eyes on the algorithm?"

"Yes. As best we can tell, it is attempting to reach a portal," the answer came back.

"Ensure that it never reaches the portal, Victor. The humans on board are to be kept alive at all costs. If they die, the algorithm dies with them."

"Yes, Master. It will be done."

The connection ended, and the AllSeer was forced to smile. The slave in the room averted his eyes, staring at the ground rather than look at something so gruesome.

The AllSeer could not ask for better news. He couldn't have planned a greater outcome.

The universe itself was bending to his will, and very soon, his lifelong ambitions would bear their fruit.

CHAPTER THIRTEEN

The first of many tests was upon the group, though only Monk knew it. Over the many years the machines had harbored the algorithm, one species above all others consistently got closest to taking it. Monk—for simplicity, the machine had adopted the name given to him by Ares—didn't know the species' name, only its leader.

The AllSeer. The being's name was known throughout hundreds if not thousands of galaxies. Even the machines knew it, and if they'd feared any creature, it was he.

Monk had thought any number of groups might come for them, though the probability was always greatest that it would be the AllSeer's minions.

"AI," Monk said from the bridge, "please bring the humans here as quickly as possible."

A few minutes passed as Monk watched the unfolding of ships reaching this dimension. The humans stepped onto the bridge as the third and hopefully final ship arrived.

"Who are they?" Veena asked as she sat down in the captain's chair and took command of the bridge.

Monk didn't move but watched as ships started toward theirs. He'd known there would be many tribulations on this journey, but he had hoped they would not meet this creature so quickly. Only *he* possessed ships like the ones Monk now saw. They were not under any kind of stealth technology. No, their arrogance was such that they would simply attempt to take the algorithm in full view.

"Monk," Ares snapped. "Who is that?"

"His name was once Alexander de Finita," Monk said in his mechanical voice.

"That's imposs—" Ares started but abruptly stopped.

Veena spoke from her chair. "The first one, not the current Ascendant. The AllSeer. Monk, is he on that ship?"

"I doubt it," Monk answered. "The AllSeer hasn't left his planet in hundreds of years. His minions do his bidding."

"What do they want?" Ares asked, although the answer was obvious to everyone on the bridge.

"He wants the algorithm." Monk turned from the screens and faced the two humans. The machine didn't know if this was the best humanity had to offer. He wasn't even sure they were the best that had ever made it to his homeworld. The machines, as well as the universe, had run out of time, though, and this was what he had to work with. "He will keep you alive until he has it, then he will kill you."

"How does he get it out of us?" Ares asked.

"Invasively," Monk answered.

Ares didn't like the idea of being invaded, but he did like the idea of being kept alive. It meant he could do a lot of killing before they finally captured him, and that was just what he planned to do.

Their ship was too large to bank sharply, but Veena was doing her damndest to knock him off his feet as he rushed back to his quarters.

The crazy bitch was jumping in and out of the third dimension, then going up to the fourth before diving back down into the third in an attempt to lose the AllSeer.

What it did to Ares was making him want to kill her.

He reached his room just as she jumped up to the fourth. His bones vibrated with the intensity of it. "AI, tell her to calm the fuck down."

Ares didn't know if the intelligence would deliver the message, but this was ridiculous. His head hurt from all the maneuvers.

He stepped into his boots and the suit folded up across his body, the dark-red armor covering all human aspects except his head. He kept the helmet retracted.

Ares grabbed the Whip from his nightstand. "Ready, old buddy?"

He could sense the Whip's anxiety and it sensed his. Both were ready for battle. That was what Ares had been born to do. What his father had raised him to do.

Veena's voice came over the intercom. "I can keep bouncing, but it's not going to keep them at bay much longer. Maybe another hour. What do you want to do?"

Ares hooked his Whip to his belt and looked at the speaker. "Let them come."

"They won't board us," Monk had explained. "We'll board them."

Ares hadn't understood what the machine meant then, but when their ship passed through the other's membrane, he got it.

They were going to place Veena and Ares' ship right in their docking bay, and once Veena quit bouncing across dimensions, there wasn't anything they could do to stop it. The technology that pulled their ship was unlike anything Ares had ever witnessed, let alone the membrane that allowed them to move through the enemy's ship.

"What now?" Ares asked as the ship finally set down, the transparent shell of the enemy's ship turning opaque once again. Veena and Monk were behind him as he stood in his suit, waiting in their own bay. "You have any plan for how to deal with this guy, Monk?"

"My best advice would be to stay alive," the robot responded.

"Every utterance makes me wish we'd left you on your planet, Monk."

"Good. That means I'm doing my job."

"They can't kill me, right?" Ares double-checked.

"If they kill either of you, the algorithm dies with you," Monk said. "The AllSeer will know that."

The bay door started to open, the enemy clearly having control of it. Monk rolled to the side of the dock. "Veena, go with him. Don't try to cover me. If I fall, we'll figure out another way."

Veena did something different then, surprising Ares.

She reached up and grabbed the back of his head, his hair shaggy now from going so long without cutting it. "Do what the robot says. Stay alive." She gave his hair a slight pull, then released him and trotted over to Monk.

The bay door finished its ascent. Ares rolled his helmet over his head, and with a flick of his wrist, sent his Whip alight.

The creatures in front of him...the only thing he'd ever seen that compared were the gigantes, though these things were more human.

All the same, they were giants, even bigger than Alistair after his mutation.

Ares' father flashed through his mind, and he saw the stern face that had raised him to be the man he was now. Giant or human, he would make them bleed.

There were three of them at the docking bay, all marching forward with an arrogance that worked to Ares' advantage.

He took two running steps and launched into the air, heading for the enemy on the far right. He reached the apex of the jump and began his fall, stretching his body out. The minion had stopped walking and was staring as if he couldn't quite believe what he was seeing.

Ares' Whip slipped through the man's core, and the moment it came through the other side, he tucked and rolled, somersaulting back onto his feet.

The giant remained standing for a moment, then his legs collapsed, and the top half of his body tumbled to the deck.

Ares hadn't stopped moving, his crimson Whip a blur of lasers.

The two giants finally quit staring, their arrogance falling away about the same time their compatriot's torso hit the deck.

They each held two short sabers. They were forced to give ground beneath Ares' ferocious attack. Monk had been right; they couldn't kill him, or they wouldn't have given up so much space.

Ares twirled down, causing both to jump, and using the multiplier of his suit, raised his Whip, twirling once more.

He caught one enemy's arm. His Whip wrapped around it and he pulled, slicing it off at the elbow. The flesh seared and the creature paused, his mouth twisted into a horrific silent scream.

That was all Ares needed. He was on his feet and shoving his Whip forward, the three strands one now. He plunged it through the man's chest, his head facing the remaining enemy.

Ares yanked the Whip out and turned his full attention to the last one—until he heard the footsteps.

He glanced to his left, his HUD counting. Ten more. Their sabers were drawn.

"Enough."

The voice was that of a god. Ares took a few steps back, assessing the new situation. The ten newcomers parted in the middle and the one who'd spoken stepped through. He was bigger than the rest, which was to say he looked more mountain than man.

He stopped just beyond the last of his soldiers. "There is nowhere for you to go. There is nothing for you to do, Titan. I've thousands of Superiors on this ship, and I'll send every single one of them at you until you yield. You'll lose limbs, organs, and anything else necessary, but I'll make sure you stay alive. We both know what I want, and we both know that I'm going to have it."

The mountain glanced at Monk.

"Doubtlessly, the machine has told you." His eyes fell on Veena. "I promise that whatever happens to you as I send my Superiors will happen to her too. Every limb you lose, she'll lose as well."

Veena stepped away from the wall. "Go fuck yourself."

Ares had no doubt that Veena would fight until death, but it wasn't chivalry that made him stop. Veena was a warrior like him, if in a different discipline.

He thought back to the beasts in the woods where he and his friend had nearly died because of being overzealous and not waiting until the right time. If he lost now, there was no hope of making it back to Earth. The mountain was right; they couldn't kill him or Veena, but they could remove the tools they'd need later. The tools they'd need to fight.

"What will it be?" the mountain asked. He looked at the two dead minions lying in multiple pieces on the deck. "You fight well, even if we're handicapped by our current predicament." He looked at Ares again. "Lay your weapon down, and you can travel as our guests until you reach the end destination. Otherwise, we can continue this dance."

Ares turned to Veena.

She nodded.

Monk was still.

Ares knelt and silenced his Whip before placing it on the deck. The remaining attacker approached as Ares stood. He bent down to grab the Whip, and it took every-thing in the Titan to not dent his head with the suit's boot.

Ares retracted his helmet and looked at the mountain. "What happens next?"

A not exactly cruel smile spread over the man's face. "That depends on you two. If you behave with dignity, you'll be treated well. If you behave like the majority of your species, we can make your trip much more painful." He gestured at Monk. "Subdue the machine, but don't break it. The master will want to inspect it."

Five men crossed the bay and surrounded Monk. The robot did nothing, simply turned his head to look at each of the five as if memorizing them.

One placed a cloth-like necklace on Monk, and a bright green ribbon lit up as it touched the droid's body. The one that had placed the necklace moved back toward the main group, and the robot followed without a word.

All three of us are subdued now, Ares thought as Veena stepped up next to him.

"Two out of three ain't bad," she whispered.

The mountain's voice silenced Veena's. "You can call me Victor. I serve my master, who I'm sure you've heard of—the AllSeer. It's him we're going to see. Come with me, and I'll show you where you'll stay during our trip."

"For an evil man," Veena whispered as they started walking, "he's got manners."

CHAPTER FOURTEEN

"You traded your souls for a shiny object, and now you have neither."

The losses had been many, more than Petra had thought possible, but the Terram had been subdued.

Her Primus spoke in a massive below-ground chamber, the remaining Terram imprisoned beneath him or in other chambers throughout their labyrinth.

Petra stood on one of the ledges, staring down at the Terram and listening to Jovan speak. The Terram were mixed with the Plutonians Kane hadn't taken with him. Petra realized, as she was sure her Primus did, that if something didn't happen quickly, disease would take over in a mass like this that was forced to live in close quarters.

Petra didn't think anyone was very worried about that.

The rest of the battle had taken four long days, but finally the Terram had sent word that they were surrendering. While they'd done that before, it seemed the Ascendant had to make a different judgment call now. His army's size had decreased by more than he'd allowed for, and to continue to fight in these holes would just decrease it more. He had to have *something* left when Kane arrived.

Even Hector had been glad to end the battles, and he'd fought like a man possessed.

Petra stood next to him, both staring down at the huddled masses.

Perhaps at the end of this battle, there would be a tally of enemy killed, but as far as boots on the ground, no one had any doubt as to whose group had done the most damage: *his*.

To Petra, it'd seemed like they'd been in constant motion. Any time an uprising that might threaten the Commonwealth's advance became visible, Hector turned his group toward it. They fought them from the side, head-on—any way that Hector could help turn the tide.

Which was what he had done.

He'd turned tides, and from what Petra had seen, it had been heroic as the saying indicated. Tides were moon-born waves that could only be turned by time, and that was what it looked like each time they showed up to fight—that it was impossible to change what was going to happen without a force of nature.

Hector had been that force of nature. When he arrived, tides changed as consistently as they did with the moon. The Primus was speaking to the defeated masses, but the word was starting to spread about where the real power stood.

Right now, it was next to Petra. Hector seemed to either stick around her or keep her near him. The result was the same; they were rarely separated.

Petra wasn't looking forward to what came next. The

Imperial Ascendant had scheduled time with her, but she didn't know what he would ask. More, she didn't know what Hector would think. Would he attempt to kill her? Petra had no illusions about how she'd fare in a fight with the man.

Either way, she knew where her duty lay—to the Commonwealth and the Imperial Ascendant.

She leaned closer to Hector. "I have to leave."

He didn't look down at her but said, "Go give your report, Bird."

She looked at him quizzically for a moment. He knew, but why did that surprise her? He knew more than she'd ever imagined. The man was in tune with everything around him almost all the time.

Petra said nothing but stepped away from the ledge. As she walked down the tunnels, her Primus' booming voice faded.

If she was honest with herself, she'd forgotten about the Ascendant during the past few months, especially the past week. Her mind had been thrust into war, and it had been worse than she'd thought it would be. Petra had heard war stories and seen holovids of fictional tales, but *nothing* could capture the sheer violence. The bodies, the screams of the dying, the sobs, the begging, and opposite that, the rush of brutal battles. All those things had kept her away from the Imperial Ascendant's original mission.

Watch Hector.

As she reached the room that contained the communication box, she tried to reframe her mind. The war was out there. In here, she needed to remember everything she'd seen about Hector.

A thought fluttered into her mind. *Am I a traitor?*

It was an odd idea and one she didn't like. She couldn't be a traitor because she was doing the Imperial Ascendant's will. Who was she turning on? Hector? A usurper?

Petra shook her head and shoved the thought away as she slipped inside the box.

She'd never been in one of these. Given that she'd lived her entire life on Earth, there'd been no need for one.

The box turned black around her, and she couldn't see outside it.

She heard the Ascendant's voice a moment later. "Petra de Osimian, I take it you managed to stay alive?"

"Yes, my liege," she responded, not sure if she was doing everything correctly.

"I've gotten reports, and it's quite clear the Terram fought hard. We lost more than I'd expected, and it's going to make the coming battle that much harder." Petra heard the Ascendant sigh; it sounded as if his breath was inside the box. "Tell me, what news is there about Hector?"

"He's perceptive, my liege, more so than I thought possible. I imagine he knows I'm speaking to you now, though not through anything I've said."

"And," de Finita said, "what has *he* said?"

"Nothing regarding you, my liege. His main concern—perhaps his only concern—is war, at least right now. It's hard to explain, but even Titans have lives outside of their duty. We go home. We have friends. Family. He seems to have none of those outside of his grandfather, though I don't think he's spoken to the man since we boarded the ships. At least, I haven't seen it." She paused, realizing she was losing herself in a torrent of words.

"What I'm trying to say, my liege, is that he is not like the other Titans or me. His life is this. He seems to have been born for war."

The Imperial Ascendant was quiet for long moments, and Petra began to wonder if she'd said the wrong thing.

"And the rest, Petra?" he interrupted her self-doubt. "Are they seeing the same thing? Is it becoming known how great a warrior he is?"

"Undoubtedly," she answered. "You can't help but see what he's doing. I'd venture to say that if he wasn't here, we might not have taken the planet. He was that valuable in the assaults."

"A single man?" the Ascendant asked.

"I know it seems hard to believe, but wherever he goes, people fight harder."

"Okay," the Ascendant said. "Stay by his side. You say he knows why you're there, so there seems to be no harm in it. Has he intimated that he might harm you?"

"No, my liege. Nothing like that."

Another moment of silence as the Ascendant thought. "Kane will arrive in the next few days. I want you to ensure that he and Hector meet each other in battle. One of them is not going to walk away from it, and I'll handle the other when they return to the Solar System."

"Yes, my liege."

"Thank you, Petra. One People. One Purpose."

"One People. One Purpose."

The box cleared, and Petra could see out again. The conversation with the Ascendant had been fast, but she'd understood what de Finita was trying to assess. How much control was Hector gaining over the military?

He hadn't come out and asked, but Petra doubted she was his only eyes here.

She remained in the box for a few minutes. She wasn't worried about getting Hector to find Kane. Hector would take care of that on his own. From what Petra'd seen, he'd never shirk a battle, and she thought he *wanted* to face the former Titan.

Petra had watched holovids of Kane, both before and after his mutation. After fighting next to Hector, she thought this insurrection would be over shortly.

It was the next part she was starting to worry about. What would happen to the Commonwealth when they returned to Earth? If Kane was as good as dead, would there be a civil war between Mars and Earth?

As far as Petra was concerned, Alistair Kane was a dead man walking.

The Ascendant finished his discussion with Petra de Osimian and stepped out of the box on his side. Had Aurelius de Finita faced such challenges in his rise? Alexander didn't think so. Back then, things had been simpler. When he had taken over the planet, the technological advances were barely out of the Stone Age, relatively speaking. The people he'd fought had been doing little more than throwing sticks and rocks at one another.

Alexander was facing multiple threats from various galaxies and mutants that Aurelius hadn't dreamed of when he was alive. The first Ascendant hadn't known what his children would end up becoming or about the monster Caius had created.

What Petra had told Alexander had been pretty much what he'd thought would happen. It was the main reason he'd placed the woman there—because he needed to gauge how quickly the military was turning to see the man as their leader.

Hector might have violence, but Alexander had brainpower. Let him defeat Kane out there; the two-month ride back would be a long time, and his feats would begin to fade. Alexander had a propaganda ministry that would begin spreading rumors the moment this insurrection was over. Right now, he needed the brute to kill Kane. Once that was finished, he would worry about the second half of this coup.

He'd watched Hector's feats in those tunnels, and combined with what he'd seen against his own Titans, Alexander thought Kane's chance of survival was low. Even the Fathers hadn't been able to see this stallion's coming, changing the battlefield so easily.

Alexander headed to the Fathers; he needed to tell them about the victory on Phoenix, then have them decide it was time for the third phase in their evolution.

He rose to the orb's chamber, stepping off the small platform and moving toward his ancestors. He went to a knee and bowed his head. "One People. One Purpose... Fathers, we've conquered the Terram and are in control of their portal, and Kane is on the way."

The dot on the orb spread out in a line. "We're receiving details now. You think Hector de Gracilis will be able to stop him?"

"I'm not sure there's ever been another warrior like him in human history. I think he'll lay waste to the entire insurrection."

The orb didn't respond but paused as it did its near-uncountable calculations. "Indeed, the entrance of de Gracilis does change the probability of defeating Kane, especially given the new data from Phoenix. You've done well in your strategy. Perhaps the Commonwealth will yet survive."

"That's why I'm here, Fathers," Alexander said. "We're ready for stage three of the Commonwealth's evolution."

A dreadful silence fell over the room. Alexander didn't know if they were double-checking him or simply thought his timing was ill-advised.

Eventually, the orb spoke. "The worlds are ready?"

"Yes, three of them. Seven more are being prepared, but we can begin with three."

It was the one piece of data that had not been given to the Fathers for security reasons. While they were aware of the third evolution, they couldn't know about its progress, not until the time to begin had come.

"Has there been word of the algorithm, Alexander?" they asked as one.

Alexander slowly rose to his feet. "Not for a thousand years."

Another moment of quiet. Alexander knew they were calculating, trying to find all the holes in this plan and the possibilities for failure.

"There's been no word from the search parties we've sent either. The last one was sent in your grandfather's time, a hundred years ago. It was lost ten years after we sent it. The risk, as we're sure you're aware, is whether this is the correct time. With no word on the algorithm for a thousand years, don't you think we're relatively safe until this danger has passed?"

"No." Alexander shook his head. "We began this evolution forty years ago for the very reason that we don't *know* where the algorithm is. I know the specifications needed to ensure that it can't harm us again, and we've reached the minimum. The process of moving you will take six months, and it's my recommendation that we start now."

He swallowed.

"I don't think *you* are taking the threat of the algorithm seriously enough, just as you thought I wasn't with the former Titan. Kane is becoming less of a threat with each kilometer he moves toward Phoenix, but the algorithm is still out there. We don't know where. Once we finalize this new phase, even if it somehow returns, it won't be able to harm you. The algorithm is the greatest existential threat the Commonwealth faces right now. It's my job to shepherd us all forward. It's time to start the final stage."

"Go ahead, then. Begin preparations. One People. One Purpose."

THE WRITTEN HISTORY OF THE GREAT INSURRECTION

There are many problems when one is fighting a galaxies-spanning insurrection against the largest government mankind has ever known; I've detailed many of them in here.

However, one I haven't spoken about is the amount one doesn't know.

For future generations that want to do as we've done, that's something you're going to want to recognize early. We didn't understand it. Whatever you think you know or are certain of, understand there is at least ten times that much information that you don't even know exists, so you can't prepare for it.

Most of it will work against you, as it has us.

It's not what you know that will kill you, at least most of the time.

It's what you don't know. It might be too late for us.

Only the gods can say for certain.

CHAPTER FIFTEEN

"I haven't seen a battle like this in over two centuries," Victor said.

Almost twenty-fours had passed since Ares gave up his Whip, and his captor was being true to his word. He and Veena were being treated with respect, though Ares didn't fully understand why.

He was coming to understand other things about this strange species. He would never consider them human; they simply weren't. He didn't know what they were composed of, but they weren't flesh and blood like him or Veena. Some flesh and blood, yes, but the flesh beneath the armor he'd worn was hard in reality and metaphorically. Scars from untold battles covered Victor's face, but it also appeared to have armor *in* it, as if it were intertwined with metal. The scars didn't appear to be flesh either, looking as if something had covered the cuts.

Ares now knew they thought of themselves as Superior, nothing else. Not human, not *the* Superior. Just Superior, a species separate from humanity, or perhaps an evolution of it. Ares had wanted to ask more questions, but Veena finally got him to stop.

"Don't wear out your welcome," she'd whispered harshly. "We've got a long way to go, and your questions are bound to start annoying him. They're already annoying me."

Ares had shut up then.

He hadn't seen Monk since they'd been taken, and at first, he'd felt a twinge of guilt about that. Then he'd realized those machines had closed up an entire planet, so the robot could probably handle himself.

He, Veena, and Victor were now in Victor's quarters, which were nicer than anything Ares had ever seen inside a spaceship. He couldn't begin to understand the tech in this place, from the membrane that their ship had passed through to the visuals he was seeing.

They were nanotech constructs of some sort, though that was all he understood about it. The tech moved so quickly he couldn't see it until it finally stopped, and Victor was able to direct it with a flick of his hand.

Ares was staring at two separate screens, one to the right of Victor, the other to the left. The Superior sat in a chair that had formed under him as he took a seat. The first time Ares had seen it happen, he'd thought the giant was going to fall on his ass.

Veena and Ares stood to his left and right. Victor never showed any sign that he was worried about being attacked, and without his Whip and armor, Ares didn't consider it either. The creature was beyond what he could do with just his body.

On the right screen, Ares was looking at Phoenix, the planet Alistair had originally fled to.

On the left, he was looking at Alistair's current fleet.

"The battle should commence in another twenty-four hours or so," Victor explained. "The Commonwealth arrived two weeks ago and, from what we can tell, took the planet in its entirety. The prophesied one is on his way to retake it."

"What in hades happened?" Veena whispered, then, speaking louder, she asked, "Why did the Commonwealth return, and why would Kane go back?"

"Much has changed since you two were involved. The Terram pledged fealty to the prophesied one. He has an army that can challenge the Commonwealth, at least on the edge planets, if not the inner sanctum."

"Obviously." Ares stared in amazement at what Alistair had managed to do. His fleet appeared to be as large as the Commonwealth's floating over Phoenix. "Why do you keep calling him the prophesied one?"

Victor didn't look around as he spoke but stared at the nanotech screens as if studying them. "The AllMother prophesied he would come. She's been searching for him her whole life. If you believe her, everything that happened with the Commonwealth was meant to happen, so he was prophesied."

Ares couldn't help but ask another question. "And you? What do you believe?"

"He will be wiped from the universe, and the AllMother will meet her fate in my master."

It was the first time he'd heard anger in the creature's voice, or something very similar to it—a steel-like quality.

"What part do we play in this?" Veena asked. "Are we heading there to the war?"

"No," Victor responded, his voice returning to normal. "I just think this battle will be a spectacle to watch. My master has plans for you that I'm not privy to. My job is to make sure you reach him safely."

"When will that be?" Veena asked.

"Enough questions," Victor said affably. He stood. "I have work that must be done." He moved his hands, and the screens disappeared from view. The door to his quarters opened, and someone who appeared human stood outside the room. Ares understood those people were slaves, and while Victor treated them well, he'd seen others treat them harshly. There were personality differences between the Superior, though Ares didn't understand them.

"Please take them to their room," Victor said.

"Yes, master," the slave responded.

Veena sat on one side of the room, and Ares sat on the other.

She looked down at her feet, pressing them alternately against the floor. It had a sponge-like quality to it she didn't understand, but it kept her interested when she didn't want to consider anything else.

Which was becoming more and more often.

She found herself concentrating on the tech around her or the algorithm in her head. Anything else, and she was afraid she would lose it.

Veena had never felt like that in her life. Her mind had always been solid, but since the machine world, things had changed for her.

Ares looked up from his cot. "You remember when the Imperial Ascendant showed us the bodies floating in the vats? The twins?"

"It'd be hard to forget a thing like that."

"That's who we're going to, right? The male? The first Alexander?"

She nodded without looking at him. "Yeah, it would seem so."

"Do you see any way out of this?" Ares asked. "Could you pilot this ship if we got loose?"

"Ha! No. This ship is unlike any other in the universe, and let's not forget there are more besides us aboard." She shook her head. "There's no escaping this ship."

"I don't think there's any bargaining with these creatures, either," Ares sounded as if he might be talking to himself. "So we're in quite a conundrum. Or we're just fucked. I don't know which."

"Are you dreaming?" Veena asked. "Have you been dreaming since we left the machine world?" She glanced at Ares as he looked up.

"No. I had the dreams when I was there—or whatever they were. I saw my father a lot, but nothing since then. Why? You are?"

"Every time I close my eyes," she answered, "my parents are there."

"Did you dream about them before?"

Veena shook her head. "I've hardly thought about them

since they died. This isn't me; it's something those machines did."

Ares raised an eyebrow. "What are you saying?"

"The same way they implanted this algorithm in us, they did something similar with my parents." She looked back at her feet, shaking her head. "I don't understand it, but I know I shouldn't be seeing my parents like this."

"Do you not want to see them?"

"There's nothing I want less in the universe. I can't even focus on the fact that we're fucked right now because I know when I close my eyes, I'm going to see them."

"I'm not trying to criticize you, Veena, but it might not be the time to relive childhood dramas. We've got a pretty good host at the moment, but I think it's going to get a lot worse fairly quickly. I need you here mentally as well as physically."

She nodded, trying to gather herself. "I know. I know you do. I'm trying. I just don't understand this. Why would they put something like this in me? I don't understand the point."

CHAPTER SIXTEEN

How many times have I thought this? Faitrin wondered. *That we had no chance? He's always gotten us through. He'll do it again.*

Faitrin forced herself to think those things because what she saw in front of her wasn't destroyable. She didn't understand how she'd forgotten the Commonwealth's fleet. She'd been a pilot for years, and looking at the force hanging over Phoenix...

I've thought this before. I've seen impossible things, but he's brought us through.

Yet, she didn't need to be harmonized with her dreadnought to know this was bigger than the Ice Queen's fleet. They'd brought everything, and now they controlled the planet. Prometheus' force was three hundred thousand kilometers away, but they'd soon be there.

Faitrin's eyes were gray since she was harmonized with everything going on inside the ship.

She switched to Thoreaux's comm.

Can you meet me in our room?

It took a second, but she heard his voice in her head. *Does it need to be now? We've got a lot going on.*

I need you.

Meet me there in ten minutes, he immediately responded.

If they died soon, she wasn't upset about the decision she made back at Pluto. She'd never thought she'd meet a leader like Pro or have a love like Thoreaux.

Jeeves, she said, switching controls. *I'll be back shortly*.

Yes, madam, the AI said. His voice was subdued too; perhaps he was the only one who understood what was coming. He was able to calculate everything at once, and these odds…

Insurmountable, she thought as she left the bridge.

Faitrin hustled back to her room, getting there a few minutes before Thoreaux. She needed to figure out her words.

When her lover entered, she saw the stress on his face. He had been thin, but he'd lost weight over the past two weeks—probably ten pounds, but she didn't want to ask. She likely looked about the same.

She was sitting on their shared bed, and he was about to begin pacing but halted when he saw her face.

"What is it?"

"We can't beat them," Faitrin whispered.

He said nothing as the door slid shut behind him.

"That force out there; it's unlike anything we've seen. We've never attacked a planet that knew we were coming. Even against the Ice Queen, we had the planet. We're going to be fired on soon, and we'll lose a lot of our ships. When we attempt to breach the planet, we'll lose more. Beneath ground? We won't have enough firepower."

Thoreaux stepped across the room and sat down next to her. He leaned forward, putting his head in his hands. "I don't know what to do. I honestly don't."

"Have you spoken to him?" she asked, the "him" not needing to be specified.

"No. He's in his thinking phase. Any time I try, he says to just keep strategizing for the landing. The only time I've seen him out of his room is in the sparring room, but he's not even practicing. Just swinging his Whip around each of his shoulders, like he's lost in thought."

"You've got to talk to him. If we go head-on, we're dead. Jeeves hasn't said anything, but he knows it too. They have too much firepower. I've slowed everything down to give us another twelve hours before we're within range."

Thoreaux straightened. "Okay. I'll go to him, but I don't know what good it'll do."

"You have to try," she whispered. "Sooner rather than later."

Thoreaux leaned over and kissed her cheek. "I'll go now. I love you."

"I love you too."

He stood and left the room. Tears rested in Faitrin's eyes, but she didn't have time for emotions. She waited for a minute or so, then stood and walked back to a bridge that was more scared than she.

Alistair understood what he'd been—an absent leader.

He'd given everyone their jobs and then disappeared.

He'd been in brief contact with Aspen, but even that had mostly been absent.

Because he knew what he was heading toward: complete and total annihilation.

It didn't matter who he prepared or what he did. He'd seen the force. He didn't have to ask Jeeves or anyone else the chances. They were zero—and he hadn't been able to figure out a way to change the paradigm. De Finita had played this beautifully; perhaps in the beginning he'd rushed, or perhaps Alistair had too many advantages in possessing the planets.

Now, he wasn't fortified.

An hour ago, he'd gone to the AllMother.

When the Ice Queen was coming, she'd taught him what he needed to know. She'd been as absent as he since then, though, and he'd thought it was because of how much of herself she'd used.

He was at the end of his rope, though, and there wasn't anyone else to turn to.

He'd come up with the briefest spark of an idea, but it wouldn't work either.

He found her in her room, a DataTrack projecting a book but discarded on her bed. She had a screen up in front of her and was staring at the Commonwealth's fleet, magnified so that one could see the awesome force.

He stepped inside, and the door closed behind him. She didn't turn to look at him, just said, "It's amazing, isn't it? What my father started and what it's become. Just looking strikes me with awe."

"That's why I'm here."

"I know," she said. "The crazy thing is, the warriors

aren't even on those ships anymore—or at least, the foot soldiers aren't. They've already taken the planet. *That* is simply the space force. Too bad they'd shoot us down before we could board them, huh?"

He moved over to a chair in the corner of the room and took a seat. He was quiet for a few minutes, staring at the fleet. The AllMother said nothing either.

He finally worked up the nerve to ask the first question. "We've always been honest with each other, Mother. I need to know honestly, do you think we're done?"

Alistair could see her profile and watched as a smirk appeared on the right side of her face. "What do you mean by 'done,' Prometheus?"

"You're staring at it. You just explained it all in a few sentences. Do you think this is the end?"

Her smirk blossomed into a smile. "Do you remember when we were heading to that dreadnought, and I told you a bit about myself?"

He nodded. "I do."

"The good thing about being ancient and still having your memory is that you have a story for everything. I don't know if this one is the right story, but I'll tell it if you want to listen."

How much have you grown, Allie? Luna's voice asked him. *In the beginning, you barely wanted to be around this woman, and now you crave her advice.*

"I'll listen as long as you talk, Mother."

CHAPTER SEVENTEEN

Only two people alive understood the story she told: her and her brother. Everyone else was dead.

It took a long time, but Alexandria was finally starting to think of herself as the AllMother. She was a little over a hundred years old and finally felt she was starting to learn how the universe worked.

Or that was what she had thought.

Much, much later, the AllMother would realize she'd spent the beginning of her life running from her brother. She couldn't mount any sort of insurrection because she was simply staying alive.

When it was happening, though, she didn't understand that.

At a little over a hundred years old, she appeared to be in her mid-thirties, and she'd blossomed into a beautiful woman. However, she only paid attention to such things when it helped her move forward. Men could be simple creatures, after all.

None of that mattered at the time of this story, though.

It was all background she gave Alistair so he'd understand she wasn't the same person then she was now.

Alexander, her brother and first of his name, had found her.

All of her deception and strategy had been for naught. Her brother had left Earth because, in his mind, nothing would matter until he possessed her.

The AllMother had thought she was too far away. She'd thought she was too clever, but while she'd been building a movement, her brother had been building technology and creatures so close to him they were almost indistinguishable.

"Another sector's down," the AllMother's second in command said.

When the AllSeer's fleet dropped into the third dimension, they'd retreated to a bunker beneath the ground, hoping to command the battle from there. It wasn't what the AllMother wanted, but she now understood the need to remain alive. Others could die, but if she did, the movement ended.

She and her council had attempted to beat her brother back. The planet was fortified, and she had an army.

Yet she was losing, and the second sector to go off the grid showed that soon, all would be lost. There were five sectors in total, and her brother was attacking the power grid, destroying her ability to attack beyond her foot soldiers.

The AllMother's soldiers couldn't withstand her brother's. They were very nearly a different species.

Twelve people were inside the bunker, each of them with a critical task in front of them. Alex was the only person above the fray, trying to take it all in so she could make the right decision.

"The fourth sector is taking heavy damage," someone reported.

"How long can it hold?" she asked without looking away from the screen in front of her.

"Ten minutes tops."

Alex's screen showed the fleet. Her brother's arrogance knew no bounds. He'd put his dreadnought within her defense system's distance.

Her second in command Rankin left his command post and stepped over to her side. "It's time to consider escaping, AllMother."

Alex didn't look at him but kept her eyes on the ship.

Leave? she wondered. *Escape while everyone else here dies?*

"AllMother?" Rankin asked.

Alex let her mind go out, spreading from the bunker into the building above. She went farther like a mist laying across the land. Alex saw death. She saw her brother's beasts murdering and pillaging.

We've already lost, she thought. It didn't matter what they tried to do down here or how long the sectors held. They were done.

"It's time to go," Rankin whispered.

Alex shook her head and stood up. "No."

The room stopped its movement. The tasks were paused. Everyone had heard her speak, and they all stopped to look at her.

Alex knew there'd be times to run, to flee her brother's obsessed madness, but she also understood she couldn't escape and let everyone else die. Was her life important for the movement? Of course. Was it worth everyone else's?

No.

Alex looked at Rankin. "Begin the retreat. Get as many of ours as we can to our ships. You'll know when to launch them."

"What do you mean, we'll know?" Rankin asked. "Where are *you* going?"

"To give us some time to escape." Alex turned to the elevator and crossed the room. Everyone was still silent, unsure whether or not to question their leader.

Rankin hustled behind her, putting his hand on her shoulder as the elevator opened. "We'll find another way. *You* have to survive."

"Do as I say. I'll see you on the other side."

She stepped into the elevator and turned to see her council one more time. She didn't know if she'd survive; the other side could be where the gods live. She was proud of what they'd done, and it had been her arrogance that had set them up like this. That had allowed them to burn.

She wouldn't escape while the rest died. She'd buy them time to escape. She owed that to those who'd entrusted their lives to her.

The elevator rose to ground level. The AllMother quickly walked across the empty building and stepped into the open air. She looked at the skyline; flames burned in windows as corvettes rushed across the night sky, lasers slashing to kill those the AllMother loved.

She turned her eyes higher, seeing the dreadnought her brother resided in. It hung above her; he'd felt where she was despite her attempt to hide in the bunker. Their connection surpassed anything Alex had thought possible between two humans. It felt like more than science to her, more than technology—almost magical. She didn't understand it, but then again, she didn't have to; the proof was right above her. He was there. He had found her. He would never stop.

Neither will I, Alexander.

Her brother's dreadnought was far too large for her to see the capsule as it left, but as it drew closer to the ground, she finally saw it. He was reaching down from the heavens to bring her to him.

The capsule touched down fifty meters from her. It stood on its end, twice as tall as her and capable of fitting ten or more inside. The door slid open, a silent invitation to come meet her brother.

The world around her continued to burn. People kept dying. They needed her in a way she hadn't given to them before. They needed a sacrifice.

Alex went to the capsule and stepped inside. Silently, she sat down, letting the seat's straps wrap around her, ensuring that there would be no escape. The capsule took off, and Alex left her children behind.

It didn't take long for the capsule to reach the dreadnought. She saw nothing as she rose, only knowing she'd finally reached her destination because movement stopped.

The capsule opened, and two massive Myrmidons stood just outside. Their sabers were drawn, their faces and bodies heavily armored. The straps holding Alex released, and she stood and exited the capsule.

She walked behind one of the Myrmidons and in front of the other, the two of them guiding her to her brother.

It'd been one hundred years since she'd last seen him; she'd only heard about the changes. Rumors had fluttered through the universe about technological distortions of his DNA, furthering their father's work to make him into some kind of monster.

If the Myrmidons she'd come across were any indication, Alex wasn't sure how much of her brother was left. Perhaps none.

The walk felt like a long one, much longer than the capsule ride had been. Finally, though, the Myrmidons moved to either side of Alex, leaving her in front of double doors.

They slid into opposite sides of the wall.

Alex's brother, Alexander de Finita, the first of his name, stood in front of her. He was on the other side of the room, facing a window that allowed him to peer down at the destruction he'd caused.

"Come in, sister," he boomed. It sounded like her brother, yet *different*, as if something else was inside him.

Alex stepped through the doors. They quietly slid shut behind her, and she was alone with the man she'd been fleeing from.

"Stop what you're doing," she told him. "Stop and leave this planet, Alexander."

"The name you've chosen for yourself...I found it quite interesting. The AllMother, because you'll take anyone in, yes?" He still didn't turn to look at her. Even his stance in this room during an attack showed his ridiculous arrogance. To be in a room so close to the edge of the ship was deadly. If it took a direct hit here, he was dead.

"I'll kill us both, Alexander," she told him. "I'll tear this dreadnought apart if you don't quit."

He moved his hands behind him, crossing his forearms over one another at the small of his back. "I chose my name based on what you did. If you're everyone's mother, then I'm the one who sees the future. I see it all, Alexandria. Why do you keep running from me? With your mental abilities, you have to know I'm going to get what I want. Even now, look at all these people dying, and for what? I'm inevitable."

Alex took a few steps into the room. It was an empty space, no computers, screens, or even places to sit—just space and windows.

"Are you going to stop, or are we going to die?"

The AllSeer turned around then.

He was huge in a way Alex hadn't imagined was possible. His body bulged from his clothes as if ready to burst out. His muscles seemed ready to explode from his skin as if they couldn't be contained by anything.

His face was larger, his skull having grown with the rest of his body.

He still had the same psychopathic calm Alex had known on Earth.

"I'll stop," he said, "if you stop. Agree now to do as I want, and everything happening beneath us will end in the next few minutes."

For a brief second, Alex thought about asking what he wanted but then forced such nonsense from her mind. She hadn't come here to negotiate. If she was going to sacrifice herself, it would be a true sacrifice, not giving him what he wanted. "Enough. It seems all you know is death and destruction. So be it."

The AllMother's mind had been of a different caliber back then. She hadn't reached her zenith.

Alex now understood why this room was empty; her brother was giving her no weapons to attack him with. She didn't care.

Her mind rushed forward, and the AllSeer smiled.

He ran at her, holding no weapons either.

The two of them collided—one's mind, the other's body. Alex grabbed his arms, doing her best to stop his forward movement. His power was unlike anything she'd ever experienced. He was everywhere at once, even as she slammed his head with a force that would have snapped a lesser man's neck. He was faster than her mind, somehow able to dodge the mental power she thrust at him.

The AllSeer was gaining ground, and Alex had no doubt that when he finally reached her, she was done.

The closed doors folded like aluminum foil as she blasted through. The two Myrmidons who stood out there grabbed for their weapons, but it was too late. Alex had them. The sabers came to life, lasers springing from the hilts. She ran them through their owners as she brought them toward her.

The AllSeer saw them coming. He reached forward, and with a might Alex couldn't imagine, wrenched one of them out of her control.

Saber versus saber, the two battled. One floated in the air, wielded by an invisible hand, the other held by flesh. The AllSeer danced around her attacks, much more adept at hand-to-hand combat.

More, she thought. *I need more.*

Alex battered the windows surrounding the room; they were reinforced and took more of her concentration. The AllSeer stepped closer with each spin and parry. The windows were vibrating, shaking, but finally they cracked, then broke.

The glass flew across the room.

The AllSeer wasn't fast enough to avoid all the shards.

Alex plunged them into her brother. Five, ten, twenty pieces cut through his tough flesh and unbelievable muscle. Blood spilled from his body and splashed on the deck. He gasped, turning his head toward his sister, then fell to his knees.

The cold night air was blowing through the broken windows. Alex's hair twisted in the wind.

Her brother was in front of her, his saber hanging at his side. Rage poured from his eyes as the blood did from his body.

"It's over," she told him. "Call it off."

He said nothing, just slowly pulled one leg up so his foot was on the floor and he was on one knee. Alex should have known; she should have been able to see it coming, but she didn't. He moved too fast, with too much strength.

With glass in his body and blood covering him, the AllSeer launched himself at the AllMother. He broke through her defenses, shattering them as he grabbed her with his left hand and brought the saber up with his right.

Alex remembered what she'd told Rankin not an hour before. *You'll know when to launch them.* She could only hope he'd listened.

Alex's mind grabbed the saber, holding it at bay. Her

brother gripped her throat with his other hand and he gritted his teeth, trying to decapitate her. Alex stood tall and firm despite her brain being cut off from oxygen.

She grabbed hold of the room and—*crunch*. Every part of it suddenly bent inward, the metal twisting and the structural integrity of the dreadnought starting to crumble. She closed her eyes and wrenched harder, feeling more of the ship bending. Alarms rang not only in their cabin but across the ship, and they were losing altitude.

Gravity was exerting its hold.

Alex's vision was fading.

The saber was inching closer to her face.

She pulled at the ship to break it more and hasten its fall to the ground. They would all die.

Alex and her brother started to slide across the deck as the ship tilted downward. If the AllSeer understood what was happening around him, he didn't show it. Hate and murder were the only emotions in his eyes.

Alex gave one last push, this one at him. She thrust with all her might and finally broke his hold on her.

The two of them tumbled forward, falling through the atmosphere as the dreadnought did. Alex lost consciousness, but the last thing she remembered was that even as her brother was thrown away from her, he reached out to grab her again.

Her last thought was, *His obsession knows no end.*

Then blackness grabbed the AllMother.

CHAPTER EIGHTEEN

The AllMother was still staring at the screen in front of her, the one showing the Commonwealth's fleet. "That was the last time I saw my brother, nine hundred years ago or so."

"How did you survive?" Alistair asked. "How did either of you survive?"

"Leave that story for another day, Prometheus. Time is short right now, as you know." She smiled again. "It always seems short now, doesn't it? There's just never enough of it."

It seemed obvious what she was telling him, but he wanted to make sure. He knew his weakness was rushing into things, and this wasn't a decision to be made rashly. "So, you went on a suicide mission to save your children?"

"I didn't think of it as suicide," the AllMother responded. "I guess I figured there was a chance I would succeed, though most likely I wouldn't. I just knew it was our only chance."

She turned around then and put both arms out to the

sides. "Now look at us, more powerful than ever. Had I not made that decision, I might not have any children today."

Alistair nodded and stood up. "Okay," he said, looking at his feet.

"Did that answer your questions? I might not have given you a chance to ask them completely."

"Yeah. It did," he responded. He met her eyes. "Thank you, Mother."

She placed her hands in her lap. "Don't doubt yourself, Alistair. Even if other decisions I made in my life were arrogant or rash, I chose wisely when I chose you. Trust yourself as I trust you."

He remembered when she'd asked him to trust her. Time changed everything, he supposed.

Alistair left the AllMother, sure about what he would do and now only needing to tell his council. He'd been about to call them together when Thoreaux arrived at his door.

He stepped into the room, and Alistair understood his second in command was feeling the stress too. It looked as if all the energy in him had leaked out days ago, and he was only moving forward by sheer willpower.

"Pro," Thoreaux said before Alistair could speak, "we've got to do something. Faitrin just came to me, and she says it's impossible, that we can't beat the Commonwealth in this situation. They're too much." He paced as he spoke, a stream of consciousness running from his mouth. "I know you're thinking, but we have to do something and we need to do it soon. Now, if possible."

"Thoreaux," Alistair said, "I'm ready."

His second stopped walking, his eyes wide.

"I know what I'm going to do."

"You do?"

Alistair nodded. "Call the council together, everyone but the AllMother. Bring Aspen, too. We'll meet in one hour, and we'll begin the mission in five."

Thoreaux sighed, relief growing on his face. Alistair wondered how relieved he'd feel in an hour when he heard the plan.

They were all gathered, including Aspen de Monaham, Thoreaux, Servia, Caesar, Relm, Faitrin, and Obs.

The drathe remained at Alistair's feet, lying lazily by him.

The rest sat at the circular table while Alistair stood.

"I'm sorry it took me so long," he said. "I... I see the same thing out there as you, and I couldn't figure out what to do. I'm still not one hundred percent sure, but as far as I can tell, this is the way we'll change the paradigm. Aspen, me, Obs, and a handful of Aspen's warriors are going to launch from here. We'll use an escape pod, one that'll be hard to hit from this distance, as well as from ground support. We're going to launch directly at the planet, get inside, and then create enough havoc to allow the fleet to join us."

Alistair looked at Thoreaux. He was doing his best to not show his disappointment, but Alistair could tell this wasn't the plan he'd wanted.

Alistair looked at Relm. "I want you to come too. You're short enough to move well inside their tunnels. It might be a problem for anyone else except Faitrin, but she's best utilized up here."

Relm said nothing, though he looked about as happy as Thoreaux with the idea.

Servia spoke up first. "Pro, are you sure about this?"

"It's the only way I know to change the paradigm. Right now, they control everything. When you look at that fleet, you know there's no way to approach. There's no way to attack without losing tremendous amounts of manpower. This might give us that chance."

No one said anything when he finished speaking.

The unspoken words seemed to hang in the air. *It might also kill you, Prometheus.*

"You don't want a larger force?" Thoreaux asked.

Alistair shook his head. "I want something that's mobile. The fewer we send, the harder it'll be to find us."

"Aspen," Thoreaux said, "can you give me three men or women who will go with us?"

The foreigner seemed less shaken than everyone else. Maybe it was because he hadn't been in a war before, or maybe the thought of dying was better than the thought of leading, but either way, the young man simply nodded. "Yes, my liege. I'll have them ready as soon as we're done here."

Alistair glanced down at Obs, who was also showing an odd calmness despite understanding everything that was being said. The drathe didn't even look up at him. "All right, then. If there are no other questions, let's get started. I want to leave here in three and a half standard hours, understood?"

Those at the table stood except for Caesar and Relm. It

was clear the two of them wanted to speak to Alistair, and the rest left them to it. After the room was clear, Caesar stood up. "I want to go too."

"I need you for the second wave or to bail me out if something goes wrong," Alistair explained. "You're big for those tunnels too. Just be ready for the second wave."

Caesar studied him for a few seconds, then nodded in agreement. "Okay, Pro." He looked at Relm, who was still seated, and put his huge hand on his pal's shoulder. "Little man, try not to get hurt. I won't be there to save you."

Relm gave a small smile. "Leave the killing to the professionals, big man. I'll see you when there's only work for the cleanup crew."

Caesar chuckled, then the big man walked out of the room as well.

It was only Relm, Obs, and Alistair.

Relm put his hands on the table and looked down at them. "I'm not afraid to die down there, Pro, but do we have a plan? I already know this isn't like with the gigantes. The corporation wasn't in any position to defend their turf like the Commonwealth currently is." He looked up. "*Do you have a plan?*"

"Yeah, I do."

Relm stood up. He didn't look happy, but he looked ready. "That's all I needed to hear. *Ave*, Prometheus."

Alistair watched as Relm left the room.

He did have a plan, just maybe not one Relm wanted to hear…

Or that would work.

CHAPTER NINETEEN

The escape pod's launch was far enough away that the Commonwealth could see it coming from within Phoenix.

Hector, with Petra next to him, watched it from beneath the ground. Their screen was magnified so the small object was visible. Lasers streaked through the space to try to hit it but missed each time. The object was moving in a straight line; it was coming for them.

Hector, as well as the rest of the Commonwealth, had been waiting for Kane to arrive. They'd followed his path carefully, and when his fleet began to slow, then came to a stop, it was obvious something was wrong. Some had thought he might retreat, seeing the enormous force in front of him.

Hector didn't.

He'd spent his time studying the man's past and understanding as much as he could about the former Titan. Hector understood that Kane could be reckless, though he didn't think that was why Kane wouldn't retreat. He didn't think "quit" was in the man. Kane would rather die than walk away from a fight.

"What do you think it is?" Petra asked as the two watched the streaking pod.

"It's him," Hector said without looking at her.

"Kane?"

Hector nodded, remaining silent.

"What's he think he can do with something that small?"

He wasn't sure. He doubted Kane would let another go in his stead, and he also doubted anyone else would be capable of causing the same damage. It made sense that Kane was in there, but why? "I guess he thinks if he can cause a disruption here, he might be able to get his fleet closer."

"He'd have to be insane to think that's possible. Literally insane. We hold the planet. He can't fit more than twenty people in that thing."

"Ten, tops," Hector corrected. "Maybe he *is* insane."

"Is that a good or a bad thing, ya think?" Petra asked.

"Well, for the people who go up against him directly, probably a bad thing. In the long term, insanity is no way to lead people, however."

Hector stepped away from the screen and moved across the small hewn-stone room to his armor.

Petra looked at him. "What are you doing?"

"Going to meet him."

"Didn't you just say it's bad news for the people who go up against him directly?"

Hector put his armor on, hanging it across his shoulders. "You can stay here if you'd like, Bird. The Commonwealth is better served if I'm fighting him. Fewer will die."

"Can you kill him?" Petra asked.

"Yes," Hector answered. He didn't have any doubt about that. Kane was a great warrior, but Hector had been bred for this. His grandfather might even say that his whole life had led to this point.

"Would you go if you couldn't?"

The question made Hector pause. It was one that no one had asked him before and one he'd never considered. He killed men; it was what he did.

"Yes," he told her.

It was the truth.

Live or die, Hector would meet Kane on the battlefield. He had no quit in him, either.

The ship swept sharply to the left.

Aspen felt his stomach do a somersault. He'd never been in a pod like this, let alone a situation like the one he now found himself in. Alistair had told him to get warriors, and Aspen had said he would. He'd done his best to not show any fear, but in reality, he'd wanted to jump out of his skin.

Now they were rushing through space and about to enter the fiery atmosphere before plunging to the ground, hoping Jeeves had correctly calculated the location of the access tunnel. If he was off by a meter in either direction, they were dead.

Aspen's three warriors were all females, and he'd picked them because they were smaller. They'd move more easily inside the tunnels, and he figured that what they sacrificed in strength would easily be made up by their added agility. Two had served his sister, and one had been part of his private guard.

Aspen was still trying to keep his face and emotions in check, although he was finding it difficult, given the pod's jerky movements.

He looked at the other warriors, all of them strapped down to seats in the circular pod. The drathe was the only one who looked as sick as Aspen felt. He'd been outfitted with a special harness that allowed him to lie on the floor, but the animal didn't look pleased.

Aspen's eyes fell on his three warriors, Tyra, Yelsen, and Lens. Their eyes were closed, their faces still. If they knew this was a death march, they showed no signs. They'd taken his orders solemnly.

When Aspen glanced at Relm, the young soldier was looking at him. He had a smile on his face, and Aspen briefly wondered if the man was happy-go-lucky or crazy. Relm held a MechPulse in his lap.

The pod jerked hard to the right. Relm waggled his eyebrows but said nothing.

Finally, Aspen looked at their leader. Prometheus. The restraints barely fit over his barrel chest and wide shoulders. His brown eyes remained open, staring at nothing. His face was calm; it didn't show anything even as the ship banked left.

Aspen could only assume the movement was to avoid catastrophe.

Even with the mighty warrior leading them, Aspen was certain they couldn't avoid it for long. What could five humans and a drathe do against a force like the one they faced?

What would Cristin do? Aspen thought as he closed his eyes. *The fallen Ice Queen?*

He wasn't a military strategist, but if anyone was like his sister, it was Prometheus. She was ice and he was fire, but in the end, both killed.

No one knew exactly where Alistair was going except him and Jeeves. He'd said the tunnels, but he hadn't said which one or where. He'd lived with the Terram for six months, and during that time, he had learned about the tunnels *above* the ground. The ones that allowed you to walk among the flames without being harmed.

Alistair hadn't prayed to the gods that the Commonwealth didn't know about them, but he was close to doing that. The tunnels were transparent, only on a certain part of the planet, and wouldn't show up on a heat scan, given what surrounded them. It was possible that the Commonwealth hadn't discovered them, and the Terram certainly wouldn't have volunteered the information.

If the above-ground tunnels had been taken as well?

Alistair guessed it'd been a fun ride, but when they landed, it'd be just about over.

Speaking of which, they were three minutes from that happening.

The ride was getting worse, and the pod was heating up. Sweat dripped down Alistair's face, as well as that of everyone else on the ship. The pod was shaking as well as veering left and right since the air defense lasers were shooting even more rapidly than the fleet had.

Alistair could see Aspen, though he didn't look at the man directly. He was holding it together. Alistair understood he'd have to protect him through much of this, but he'd expected that. He was here for a very specific reason, and like the AllMother, Alistair knew talent when he saw it. Perhaps it was different than his, but that was fine.

Jeeves was in Alistair's ear on a comm. "The landing isn't going to be like we wanted, sir."

"What's the difference?"

"You're about to see," the AI came back.

Alistair leaned forward, then lifted off the seat for a moment before slamming back down. He felt the pod rolling and hoped the metal legs were reaching out to bring them to a stop. Over and over they flipped.

Aspen vomited on the floor, but the mess quickly rotated to the ceiling as the pod continued to flip.

"*JEEVES, GET IT UNDER CONTROL!*" Alistair shouted.

"Trying, sir," the AI responded calmly.

The pod stopped turning but was now skidding across something that felt relatively smooth.

"We hit the tunnel?" Alistair asked, his body now pressed against the chair.

"Please give me a fucking second," Jeeves said.

The pod started slowing. Alistair gauged that through the pressure that was keeping him in his seat. It finally came to a stop, but the bottom began to vibrate.

"Broth," Relm said, "you wanna tell us what in hades is going on?"

Alistair snapped off the restraints and stood up. "Not

completely sure." He reached for Obs and took his off next. The drathe snarled at him, obviously more than a little angry at what was going on.

The vibrations increased as the rest of his crew stood up.

"Release in five seconds," Jeeves said in his ear.

"Are we alo—" He'd wanted to finish the sentence with "alone," but the floor opened beneath him, and he fell.

Alistair had his MechSuit on, and the helmet rolled over his head as he unleashed his Whip, ready for whatever was to come.

He hit a glass floor, landing for a brief second on one knee before bouncing up and rushing forward. His body automatically reacted as if enemies were there.

He spun the Whip in a tight circle around his left shoulder, then his right, but it cut only through the air.

They were alone.

"Did everyone make it?" Jeeves asked.

Alistair turned around. "Including me, we got five people plus a drathe," he said. "The tunnels appear to be empty."

"They won't be for long," Jeeves said. "Get moving."

***

As Hector had readied himself, he'd been in contact with Jovan, the Primus. He'd convinced the man to send a small group after the Titan, no more than twenty. More than that, and it would fill the tunnels with unnecessary bodies.

Petra was with him as the group of fifteen hopped onto the train that would take them to the other side of the planet. Kane had been smart about where he landed; it was well away from the majority of the Commonwealth's forces. It'd take an hour for them to get there, and while Hector had tried to convince Jovan to remove their forces on that side of the planet, he hadn't been able to.

Hector thought there would be quite a few bodies lining the tunnels by the time they arrived.

Jovan was in his ear as the train took off. "We've got a problem, Hector."

"What's that?"

"We've lost track of the pod. It's not registering in any of the tunnels. They might not have made it. We've got scout teams scouring the area on that side, but so far, there's nothing."

Hector was quiet for a moment. He knew the Titan wasn't dead. The pod had gotten too close to the planet for the defense system to take it out, and the atmospheric flames clearly weren't going to do it.

"He's alive, sir," Hector said. "We're moving forward with the expedition."

"I'll keep you up to date with anything that comes through," the Primus responded. "Good luck."

Kane was alive.

Now Hector was going to hunt him.

CHAPTER TWENTY

In another part of the universe, Ares and Veena were about to come face to face with someone they'd thought was a myth for much of their life. The story of the first Imperial Ascendant's twins had for the most part been just that, a story. It was a myth that those inside the Commonwealth grew up hearing but never speaking about or giving it much credence.

Who could live that long? It was impossible.

Until it wasn't.

Ares looked at the planet beneath them as he stood next to Victor. He and Veena both had their hands clipped now, though these restraints were different from the clips he'd used on Earth. These could restrict or remove movement in certain places at the Superior's will. Right now, only their arms were disabled, so if they'd wanted to run, it was possible.

Except there wasn't anywhere to run.

They'd ended up using a portal to get here, though it looked to have been made by the AllSeer as opposed to the

Commonwealth or other natural humans. Ares didn't ask any questions about it, and Victor didn't volunteer any answers. The closer they'd gotten to this planet, the quieter their captor became. No longer chatty, it was as if he'd taken on the personality of his master.

"Are you scared of him?" Ares asked out of earshot of anyone but the Superior and Veena.

Victor turned away from the screen. "I respect the master, but it would be detrimental not to fear him as well. He's the most powerful being in this universe, and when you see what he's done, you will plead for your life. You're not Superior, and he owes you nothing."

So, he takes this pretty seriously, Ares thought.

As they watched the planet grow bigger in front of them, their ships nearing the atmosphere, he was beginning to see manmade—or Superior-made—shapes. Not just long walls, but buildings that stretched for kilometers in every direction. Things even Earth hadn't considered doing.

Veena was quiet, and Ares didn't know if that was due to her mental issues or the awe-inspiring planet they were about to land on. Ares didn't ask. Outside of that one question, he kept his mouth shut too.

The ship touched down, and Ares found that the clip on his wrists was now affecting his legs. He couldn't move them at will anymore, but only when someone else allowed him to. He didn't know if it was Victor or another low-level Superior or all of them. His jaw and voice still worked, though he kept quiet.

The dreadnought was emptying from different hatches, and he still saw no sign of Monk. No one paid him any mind but appeared to each have something that urgently needed doing. Ares wondered if there was some kind of hive-mind going on here, though not seriously because he knew verbal communication existed between them.

Suddenly, his and Veena's legs were moving them toward an exit hatch. Victor was in front of him, and others that came and went didn't so much as look at his prisoners.

Monk joined them as they reached the exit bay. Ares thought about speaking to him, but the droid's quietness showed that might not be the best idea. Perhaps Monk couldn't speak.

As they left the ship, Ares found himself in a building constructed of material that was different from the ship's. Where the ship had some give to it, not squishy but close, this was pure metal. The black color stretched around the entire docking bay, not allowing Ares to see anything else of the planet.

His eyes come to rest on the only other person not running to and fro across the docking bay.

Ares had seen giants—true giants, the gigantes—but nothing prepared him for this person. Even a beast such as Victor looked like a cheap knockoff of what stood in front of Ares now.

He'd been a Titan, a warrior bred to fight, yet as Ares peered at the creature, he understood there would be no chance to kill him. There would be no chance to fight him. There would be no chance at anything. This creature would annihilate him with the flick of his wrist, breaking every bone in Ares' body, probably without feeling it.

If there were gods, this creature had spawned from the dark ones—their direct progeny.

He stood perhaps four meters tall, and beneath the black cloak he wore, muscle bulged.

His face was human-like but different, too. It held the same toughness Victor's had but was darker. The lines in it were from both scars and time. His brows were heavy over his eyes, which appeared black to Ares, though he couldn't be sure in this light.

This was the rumor, the myth, the thing that the Commonwealth had tried to keep from the populace. There was only one lineage of the Ascendancy, and the rest were lies or impostors. That was the story they'd put out for a thousand years, but Ares now knew for certain that had been the lie.

Alexander de Finita, the first of his name, lived.

The AllSeer stood in front of him.

The huge creature stepped over to Veena, who stood on Victor's other side. He bent down so that their faces were close.

"You did well, Victor." He cocked his head to the side as he stared into Veena's eyes. "It's in there, isn't it? The algorithm they held onto for so long. It's in your beautiful mind now, yes, Veena de Ragnimus?"

The AllSeer straightened and walked over to the other side of Victor, to Ares. He bent over so that once again, he could look a normal-sized person in the eyes. Ares saw that they were black. Completely so—no pupil, no whites, just a black orb inside his head. "Romulus de Livius. It's inside you as well. Do you truly know what you are carrying?"

Ares found he could speak, though when his voice came out, it was a whisper. "We do."

The AllSeer smiled, and as he pulled back his lips, his teeth and gums were black too. Rotten or simply made from different materials, Ares couldn't tell.

"You know nothing about what's in your head, nor about the powers that it holds. If you did, you would never have gone to that planet. You would have stayed further away from it than Veena does the memory of her parents. If you had any clue, you'd know that when you went there, you didn't sign the warrant for your death, but for your soul."

The AllSeer straightened and turned his attention to Monk. The robot was behind the group, but the AllSeer could easily see over them. "The last machine of the machine world. Did you really think that you'd keep it from me forever? Did you think that by giving it to these two, I wouldn't get to it? Out of everything in this universe, it's you machines I understand the least. For now, at least. Since I have you, I believe that's going to change."

Lastly, the AllSeer went to Victor. He placed a gorilla-sized hand on the Superior's shoulder. "You did well, my son. Go, rest, soon we leave this planet and head home."

Victor didn't show surprise, but he did ask, "Earth?"

The AllSeer nodded. "Earth."

Victor smiled and walked away from their group, Monk following him without saying a word. Ares saw no clip on him, but it was clear the machine was under Victor's control.

That left the AllSeer and the former Primuses. He stepped back so he could fully view them both. "You two are out of options. You'll never leave here. You'll die in my power, one way or another. About the only choice left to either of you is whether you want to continue living after I'm done with you or not. Until then, you don't even have that choice since I'll make sure you remain alive until I'm finished."

He turned his back on them and started walking. Ares and Veena began following about five paces behind, their legs tied to his will. Ares looked at Veena, but she didn't turn to him. She was either scared nearly to death, which Ares thought somewhat possible given the creature in front of them, or she was lost in her own head.

The AllSeer led them out of the landing bay into a tunnel that had obviously been built for his massive size. It was as black as the AllSeer's eyes and as silent as space. There was no one running around as there'd been in the bay—it was just the three of them.

The AllSeer took a left, then a right, and still Ares saw no one else.

At last, they entered a large dome that was the same color as everything else had been. Without any doubt, black was the AllSeer's favorite color—that or Ares thought he was colorblind.

The AllSeer walked to the other side of the room while Ares and Veena stopped where they were, still unable to direct their own muscles. When he reached the far wall, he turned around, and an orb appeared in the center of the room between the two groups. To Ares, it didn't appear to be a holovid, but it also didn't look physical. Ares wasn't sure what the thing was made of.

"That," the AllSeer said, "will be the end of my use of

you. On Earth, an orb very similar to that one resides. It's where I would now reside if I'd done as my father wanted. It's the AI the algorithm now in your heads created. The most powerful intelligence ever made, and one that hasn't been replicated."

The AllSeer started circling it, looking at the orb instead of them. "We are going to Earth, and I'll insert the algorithm in your minds into it." As he reached the side of the orb they stood on, he turned to face them. "You two have just entered the greatest game ever played in human history, and you're going to see fate's final twist."

It was at that point Ares finally realized the man was insane. He opened his mouth to say something but found he couldn't. The orb disappeared behind the AllSeer, the room empty and black again. "Romulus, you'll remain here until it is time to leave. I don't think I'll have much use for you until we reach Earth." He turned his attention to Veena. "Come. I may yet have a use for you."

The AllSeer and Veena left the room. Ares wasn't able to move any part of his body or see if Veena looked at him as she left. He could only stand straight and listen as the doors closed behind him.

CHAPTER TWENTY-ONE

Obs rushed through the tunnel, looking for the first exit leading into the ground. Alistair shot a quick look at the pod they'd taken. He was able to see that Jeeves had landed them as well as he could, but then something must have hit them. He could see the scratches and superficial cracks on the outer tunnel wall from where they'd tumbled across it.

Jeeves had managed to right it and the pod had drilled through the glass, creating a vacuum seal before dumping them into the tunnel.

Alistair had been right; the Commonwealth wasn't aware of the tunnels, or at least they hadn't been. He wasn't sure how long that would remain the case now that they were here.

Obs found the exit pretty quickly. The drathe had puke in his fur from Aspen's vomit and seemed very pissed about that. He'd have to get over it quickly, though, because Alistair had plans for him.

The group rushed to where Obs stood. The tunnel went

on across the planet's ground level, but at this point, the floor was made of a different material. It would usually take Terram permission for this floor to move one way or another, but Alistair didn't think he'd find anyone guarding beneath. If there were any Terram alive, they were far from this place.

"Everyone step back," Alistair said.

He didn't know if the four newcomers had ever seen this side of him, but he didn't have time to consider it. He closed his eyes, and in the blackness of his mind, he saw the floor. He searched further, finding the mechanical pieces that would move it, then he pushed on those.

He didn't open his eyes as he heard the screeching and mechanical noises of metal that didn't want to move but was being forced to. Inside the darkness, Alistair watched the plate shift beneath the ground and create a space for them to enter the planet.

When he opened his eyes, Aspen and two of his warriors were staring at him. The other was looking at the new hole in the ground.

Relm slapped Aspen's back. "You'll get used to it. Make haste, not waste. Let's go."

He stepped toward the hole and hopped inside, his pulse immediately coming up and sweeping the tunnel for enemies. "Clear!"

"I'll take the rear," Alistair told the other four.

Obs walked over to his side and the two watched as the first three warriors went down, leaving Aspen.

"I'm assuming you've got a plan for me? I'm not what my sister was with the gloves, and I'm not sure why I'm here. Those three would have listened to you as well as me."

Alistair knew he was referring to the gloves that had nearly killed him during his battle with the Ice Queen. They were to the Monaham people what Whips were to Titans.

"I've got a plan for you," Alistair affirmed. "Now go on down there. I imagine they're already sending men our way."

Aspen nodded, then dropped through the hole.

Alistair knelt next to Obs and put his head close to the animal. "You make sure Aspen stays safe at all costs, okay?"

Obs nuzzled his master.

"Go on, now," Alistair whispered.

The animal bounded to the other side.

Alistair peeled his helmet back and glanced at Relm, who was staring up at him. The man gave him a thumbs-up, and Alistair nodded in response.

He hopped over the opening and continued down the tunnel.

The door to the tunnel closed behind him, separating him from those he'd come with.

The plan was in action.

"*What's he doing?*" Aspen shouted as the tunnel's opening closed.

Prometheus had hopped over it and was now walking on top of the planet while everyone he'd brought with him was beneath it.

"Our part here is different than his," Relm said. He saw the other three warriors were looking up too, not to mention Obs. Pro hadn't lied to him; he was the only one who knew the plan. Relm thought it was insane and that they were all going to die, but this wasn't the first time he'd thought that about Pro's ideas, and here they were, still alive.

"What's our part?" Aspen snapped.

Obs let out a low growl.

"Not to stand here and bicker," Relm said. "That's part one, and he was *very* insistent on it, Aspen. If I remember correctly, he said, 'Once we get there, don't argue about shit that doesn't matter because it'll get you all killed.' So, that's the first part. Think you can manage that?"

Aspen was quiet, taking the slight tongue-lashing, and Relm was glad he had. He'd have hated to stroke him with the butt of the pulse to shut him up.

"Good." Relm stepped forward in the tunnel and listened. He didn't hear anyone yet, which meant they had time. The Terram had done a good job of hiding these above-ground things, and maybe that'd been for a reason—so Prometheus would have a way to get in. Or maybe it was an accident, Relm didn't know, and it didn't really matter. "The Terram aren't stupid. In fact, they're probably smarter than both of our ancestors combined if you look at what they built here. They're engineering geniuses, and Pro knows that."

Obs was pacing beneath the opening, angry about having been left by his master.

Relm couldn't do anything about that right now. He

knew the drathe was listening, and the only hope they had of reuniting was to follow Pro's plan.

"We know the Terram were defeated, but Pro thinks they are being kept in a few different places. One of them is where they kept us when we showed up. That's ten kilometers away from where we're standing right now, just farther down. The other two are on the other side of the planet. They only have three of these caverns big enough to house people. That puts the majority of their guards on the other side."

Obs had stopped pacing. He was looking at Relm with discerning eyes.

"There's got to be more to it," Aspen said.

"This all relies on the gods." Relm knelt down, placed his pulse on his back, and retracted the armor over his hands. He snapped his fingers and Obs walked over, letting Relm stroke the parts of his fur that were not covered in vomit. "I'm not going to sit here and say I like this plan. It's the craziest shit Pro's ever come up with, but we've all sworn allegiance, so we're doing what he tells us to. There are more tunnels in this place than you'll ever imagine, and there are tunnels beneath where the Terram are being held. We're going there, and we're waiting until he gives us a sign."

"Then what?"

Relm, looking at Obs, smiled. "Then we start an uprising."

Aspen shook his head, but Relm knew he would never have done that in Pro's presence. Not here. Not like this. But here they were.

"Do you think this will work?" Aspen asked.

"Sit, Obs," Relm whispered. The drathe did as he was told. Relm kept petting as he looked up, his eyes falling on all four soldiers. "When your sister brought her people to us, I thought we were dead. I knew it, in fact. I watched one of those white slaves you guys breed nearly kill one of my best friends in the street. He got us through that, even though it almost killed him. Do I think we'll get through this? Not a fucking chance, broth. Those people in the sky, though? They need us to try. All my friends and your whole family need us to give this every fucking thing we have, so that's what we're going to do." He stood up, his armor rolling back over his hands. "I'll be honest with you, Aspen de Monaham. If you don't want to come, sit here. Go and hide somewhere. I'm going forward, and I know this drathe is too, but you three? You can do what you please. I've got my orders."

Aspen looked at the ground for a moment, and when he looked back up, the fear had been shoved down. It wasn't gone, but it was somewhere deep inside him. He unhooked the pistol from his holster. "Let's go. Tyra, take the rear."

Obs wasn't happy with his master. He understood now why he'd been asked to leave the room when it was only Relm and Prometheus. His master had known then that he'd be separating from Obs, and he didn't want to worry about having to explain it. The drathe would have done what his master said, but here it would have taken more time, not to mention dealing with this new human named Aspen.

Obs understood it was the smart move, but it didn't soothe his annoyance too much.

Relm was in the lead, one of the new warriors behind him, then Aspen, and finally the last woman. Obs kept pace with Aspen. He'd been given his orders just like Relm and he planned on following them.

He was to keep Aspen alive at all costs, which meant his own life.

Obs didn't question that. His purpose was his master's, and if his death furthered his master's purpose, then that's the way it should be.

He didn't know what was to come, but drathe didn't think about the future. Obs could feel his master and he was still alive, though he was moving in the opposite direction. He didn't know what Alistair Kane was going to do, but unlike the humans around him, he didn't worry about that either.

His master would do what was necessary to save them all.

Obs would do his part.

Alistair was moving quickly.

He knew Thoreaux had thought he was using all his time thinking back to when he'd refused to see anyone, but that wasn't all he'd been doing. He'd been studying this massive planet with its incredible underground system of trains, tunnels, and massive cathedral-like spaces. He'd had Jeeves run thermal scans, but in the end, the AI hadn't been able to see anything beyond the fire.

So, a lot of this had been guesswork, but there wasn't anything else they could have done.

Change the paradigm.

As Alistair jogged through the transparent tunnels, a thought came to him.

The AllMother has to keep living because the old woman continues to teach.

Then Luna spoke up. *Allie, you just better keep living right now.*

A smile appeared on his face behind his helmet.

Alistair had used the trains in this place when he lived here, though seldom. The Terram didn't like him moving too much; they hadn't trusted him. They were high-speed, as easily as fast as anything on Earth, and more, they traveled almost straight to their points.

The Commonwealth wasn't dumb, and if they'd lost the pod, they at least knew the direction it was coming. They'd use the train to get here, and Alistair planned on being ready for them.

Every time he'd chased his enemy, he'd been ready to kill, except for with the Ice Queen, when he'd been forced to give himself up.

This time, he was willingly giving himself to them.

About twenty minutes after leaving his group, he found the closest entrance to the train depot. His mind moved the door and he hopped down, then took off jogging again.

He understood that speed was of the essence. If the kill squad got off that train, they'd still be hunting. Those on this side might be hunting, but there weren't as many, and he and Relm had spent the last couple of hours going over the tunnels—the ones most likely to be uninhabited, or at least with few people walking them.

All that really mattered, though, was Alistair interrupting the kill squad. Making them think he'd come alone. Then no one was going to be looking for the rest.

CHAPTER TWENTY-TWO

Ares hadn't moved for over an hour. All he'd had was his thoughts, and they weren't a great space to be in. Mainly he was mentally kicking his own ass for all this. Leaving the Commonwealth, going after the algorithm, convincing Veena every step of the way that it was the right choice.

He thought back to his father, but he could remember no lessons Adrian had taught to get him out of this. His father's teachings did nothing for him now.

Nothing did.

He heard the doors behind him open and watched as Monk rolled in with two of the Superior surrounding him. They gave him a quick glance then walked back out, leaving the two frozen entities to wait by themselves.

Ares could see Monk out of the corner of his eye, and the machine looked like it powered down once its movement stopped.

The doors shut, and a minute or so passed.

A blue light appeared on Monk's head, then the robot did a quick turn so he was staring at Ares. "I'm tempted to leave you like that. I think hearing you curse a lot when you're finally freed might be very humorous."

Ares couldn't move or say a word. He stared forward as his mind went into hyperdrive, wondering what in hades was going on.

Monk rolled so the two faced each other. "Despite the humor, I'm going to free you. You most likely are going to fall down, given how long you've been frozen, so be prepared."

The blue light blinked red, then Ares felt his muscles relax. The clip released from his arms.

He was quick enough to catch himself before he landed on his ass.

He let himself down easily, then tried to speak, but it took his jaw a few tries to work right. "What the fuck are you doing? You've had that capability all the time, and you haven't used it?"

Monk wheeled his treads so his back faced Ares. His head searched the room, including the ceiling. He said nothing.

"You have to know they're watching this room. They'll be in here in seconds, then you're going to the trash compactor, Monk. I'm not going to save you either. That was idiotic."

Monk rolled toward the middle of the room. His voice carried to Ares as he spoke. "The problem with humans is that you are an arrogant species. It blows my processing units that for thousands of years, you've considered your-self the pinnacle of evolution in one breath, yet worship a single god or multiple ones at the same time. You are not the pinnacle of evolution, just the species that has spread through the most galaxies, at least in this dimension. You may be able to travel in the higher dimensions, but you still don't have the ability to see the beings that live there."

He turned around and faced Monk. "If you created the ability to hide conversations, do you not think I can? That's what the blue light is trying to tell your small mind. We're safe right now. No one can see us, and the AllSeer hasn't decided to dig into me yet and find out what I'm capable of. The AllSeer suffers from the same human compulsions as you, apparently, thinking he knows everything. He may have mastered technology at a level the rest of your species hasn't, but he's not even out of what we consider the second evolution. So, as an old saying of your people's used to go, I have a few tricks left up my sleeve. When they return, things might change, but for now, we've got a bit of time. I'd honestly rather spend it with Veena, but I think the AllSeer has different plans for her."

Ares pushed himself back to the wall, not yet ready to stand up. He didn't need any more explanations from Monk. There was some kind of stealth mechanism over the room, and whatever tech was watching them wouldn't see anything but what the robot wanted it to. "Is Veena safe?"

"That part is up to her," Monk said. "Her family plays a larger role in her life than she knows, and I believe the AllSeer knows that as well. He sees deeply, deeper than my kind originally thought. However, it's why we've done what we've done with her. I hope she figures herself out. For now, you and I have other things to consider."

Monk rolled back to where Ares sat, coming to his right side. He kept talking, more than he ever had before. "This has the possibility to turn out better than we thought, as long as I'm not torn into parts. Leaving this up to you would be like leaving it up to a newborn. Now be quiet for one second. This part is delicate."

The room was silent for a minute or more, then the fiery planet named Phoenix appeared in the middle of the room like the orb had. It wasn't a holovid, and it looked like a planet was sitting in the middle of the room.

"Okay, these are the most dangerous parts. Hacking their restraint tech is easy, but right now, I'm hacked into what you'd call an AI and having it broadcast this here. The AI isn't as arrogant as humans, so it might notice something is going on. I'm going to do my best to keep that from happening. Either way, you won't die until you get back to Earth."

Ares' eyes narrowed as he stared at the two fleets in the image. One was farther out from the planet; it appeared to be just a bit out of firing range. Ares could tell it was far enough away that if the Commonwealth fleet gave chase, the other would have time to retreat, thus creating a standoff.

"This was why the AllSeer paused," Monk said. "What happens here is very important to him, though I'm sure he has other plans as well."

"Why is this important? If he wants to get back to Earth, what's it matter what happens with de Finita and Alistair?"

"Your former mentor is the prophesied one. Whether or not the AllSeer will admit it to himself, there is a part of him that fears the Titan. Just as the AllSeer has said that fate drives him to his destiny, the AllMother has said that the Titan would be found. It was her own fate, and she believed in it totally. If Kane survives this, it's going to change things for the AllSeer, and I believe he knows it."

"Why?" Ares asked. He didn't care about being called stupid by this machine anymore. He was far out of his element at this point, and he didn't think anyone in their mid-twenties could understand all this.

"Because I'd venture to say it's theoretically impossible to survive this. I know you're not too dumb to see that the Commonwealth's fleet is too large to be defeated. More, they have the planet." It sounded as if a smile were in the machine's voice as he continued. "Multiple galaxies are watching this right now, and I don't think *anyone* thought what just happened would. When the AllSeer saw it, he stopped everything, even his business with Veena."

The machine paused.

"Don't make me ask."

Again the smile in his voice, "But it's so much fun for me. Fine, human. An escape pod launched from Kane's fleet. It was far too fast and agile to be shot down, which is of course the point of an escape pod. It didn't flee, though. It landed on Phoenix, and no one can see inside those flames."

Ares raised his eyebrows. "Alistair launched himself alone into that planet? It wasn't a bomb or something like that?"

"He can't bomb that planet. He needs the portal, and the Terram are his responsibility. All probabilities point to him having gone, though perhaps not alone. Luckily for us, the AllSeer's tech is allowing us to see this almost in real-time. We'll know who wins as soon as it happens."

Ares rubbed his hands through his long hair. Alistair

had been the best he'd ever seen, and whatever arrogance Ares had when he served under him, he'd known it. The man was two decades older, yet able to do things mere mortals were awed by. When he'd fought him on the dreadnought, Alistair had been almost inhuman. He'd done things Ares had never imagined possible, the mutations giving him that much more.

Plus, there was the thing Ares never truly considered because he hadn't wanted to.

What had Alistair done with his *mind*? He was nearly an immortal.

"I'm waiting for you to ask me if he can win."

"I have another question first," Ares said.

Monk's head turned to him, cocked now, doing his best to display shock with his machine body. "That's surprising. I normally read you better than you read yourself. Go on, human."

"Well, you did basically invade my mind for the gods know how long, so I'll let you knowing me well slide." He pointed at the planet. "Does our plan ever put us back with Alistair?"

Monk turned his head back to the image in front of them. The humor in his voice was gone. "Telling you too much could be dangerous, and not just because you're immature and brash. There are things to come that you need not know about yet if probability holds. However, if it is the Titan's goal to return to Earth as well as yours, you would think such a thing might be possible."

Ares was quiet for a moment. All the regret he'd experienced as he waited in here alone faded. Quitting the Commonwealth, getting stuck out here—all of it disappeared because there was one regret he hadn't allowed himself to deal with. He'd ended up helping save Alistair, or at least doing the best he could, but he'd traded on his mentor. He'd bought what the Ascendant sold for so long, he nearly paid with all his soul. He regretted *that*.

Looking at what Alistair had done, he regretted not being by his side.

Could he fight one day alongside him? That was what the machine was saying. Maybe their destiny would put them back together. It was the greatest news he'd ever heard.

"One more thing, robot, then you will get the question you want."

Monk nodded. "I know this one. What does the AllSeer want with Veena?"

"Bingo." Veena was the most important person in the universe to Ares and probably would be until the moment he died. Regardless of what was in front of him, he would always be concerned for her safety.

"The AllSeer, as far as I know, has yet to create a female version of himself. All the Superior are male replicas or something close to it. The AllSeer wants a bride, but it has to be someone with the right spirit. His sister had it, of course, but despite the AllSeer's insanity, he's not incestuous. He sees the trouble in Veena's mind, and my best guess is he hopes to exploit it to create his bride. He will have his sister, his empire, and his wife, and then he will have his progeny. That's what he wants."

Ares nodded, showing no emotion. He trusted Veena. She'd see through the AllSeer's wiles. "Okay, give me your odds for Kane, then I'll give you mine."

"I can't say that I'm a creature who doesn't believe in fate because pretty much my entire time of sentience has been spent waiting for the poor excuse you turned out to be. However, you *did* show up. If fate exists, which I believe it does, I'd put him at fifty percent. Only because if he loses, I think we all lose. If it wasn't the prophesied one, zero percent." He turned his blinking head to Ares. "What say you? You know him better than I. What are his chances?"

"One hundred percent. He's got this." Ares smiled big. "I mean, can you imagine, Monk, the godsdamn parades they're going to throw for me when I show back up on Earth, reunite with my former mentor, and then destroy the whole Commonwealth? There will be statues across every galaxy known to man. I know you're excited."

Monk slowly turned back toward the planet. "For my sake, I hope Kane dies now so I never have to witness *that* travesty."

CHAPTER TWENTY-THREE

Alistair made it to the depot. It was empty, but he saw no train in it. Most likely—or so he hoped—that meant the kill squad hadn't arrived yet. Those already on this side of the planet were most likely scurrying, searching for Relm's party, but he couldn't worry about that. He had to keep his mind here in the moment, doing what he could.

He waited on one of the rock benches, rolling back his helmet and keeping his Whip in hand.

His mind tried to go to Luna, but he wouldn't let it. He couldn't go there and imagine that marriage right now.

Instead, he considered the AllMother. True, she'd been a hundred years old or so but still going up against an impossible force. She'd done it because it'd been necessary. She'd been willing to die, and Alistair *still* didn't know how she'd survived. He imagined she'd tell him one day when it was needed.

He smiled as he thought about how stupid he'd been to hate these people—the Subversives. How he thought they'd been trying to destroy the fabric of society for anarchy, for the rise of warlords. These Subversives, of which he was now one, were the greatest humans ever made. He didn't know if he deserved them, but he was glad he had them.

His eyes flicked to the right as he heard the train arriving. It was slowing down, and the air it pushed forward rushed across his bare face.

Alistair stood, not rolling his helmet up. He kept his Whip in hand but didn't unfurl it. His old friend was ready to kill, though; Alistair could tell. Its sentience felt him, and it was ready to do the business it knew so well.

The train pulled to a stop.

Alistair stepped forward.

He watched as the kill squad stepped off.

They'd seen him at the train depot since he arrived, and Petra had watched as Hector stood up, staring at the screen in front of him. Hector didn't move an inch, only stood staring at the man he'd come to kill.

They'd been getting updates, and while her Primus felt certain he wasn't by himself, they'd found no one else. Petra realized the Commonwealth's arrogance had gotten the better of them this time. They'd thought the Terram hadn't built on this side of the world, out of laziness or lack of time or something else. The fire surrounding the planet should have immediately told them that wasn't the case, but no one had thought it through.

Turned out, this side of the planet was meant for hiding, at least of some sort. The camera system wasn't as sophisticated, and the tunnels were not as plentiful on the blueprints they had. The Terram had feared the Common-wealth enough to create a protective coat over the world, then they'd built half of it to allow them to hide.

At least, that was what Petra thought. She hadn't said a word about it since they'd been on this train, but it made sense in her mind. She imagined Hector thought the same, though she didn't dare say anything to him right now.

He was radiating danger, and the closer they moved to Kane, the hotter it baked off him.

Finally, the train stopped.

The doors remained closed, and Hector turned toward them. "You may all step off, but if he attacks, no one is to join in unless I fall. If you do join in, I promise I will cut you down myself. Is that understood?"

Petra rolled her suit's helmet up and quickly scanned the room.

"We understand," she said.

"I need everyone to say it," Hector commanded.

"Understood." The response came as one.

He nodded. He took his helmet from his waist and sat it on the ground, then unsheathed his sabers, though he didn't activate them.

"Open the doors," he told the train.

He stepped off first, Petra close behind him, then made room for the rest of the troops. She moved to the far wall, her Whip in her hand, though it was also still off.

Her eyes focused on the former Titan, the former Primus, taking him in face to face for the first time.

He was smaller than Hector by a good margin, though he was by no means small. Compared to mere mortals, he was a giant. She could only see his head; the rest was covered by his suit. She remembered him, though his hair was longer now.

His eyes fell on Hector, and a madness like nothing she'd ever seen flooded Kane's face. He'd been calm before they'd stepped out. Before he'd seen Hector. He'd been calm during the train ride over as if he was a regular guy heading to work.

Now, though, that was gone, and his Whip unfurled. Red lasers began twirling in front of him.

"What's your name?" he barked across the three meters separating him from their group. He didn't sound like a god because a god could never hold so much hate against something so far beneath him. He spoke as if *they* were evil, perhaps the evilest things to ever exist, and he a knight of old meant to cast it out. He spoke as if they had no right to be here.

"Hector de Gracilis. You are Alistair Kane?" Hector's voice remained calm despite the danger that pulsed with each beat of his heart.

"Are you the man who married my wife?"

Hector looked at the ground for a second. When he looked up, he didn't smile or gloat. He said simply, "I am."

Something was going on in the former Primus' head. Petra had no idea what he was thinking, and truthfully, she'd never considered the marriage as being a factor. This had been a mission and nothing more, but understanding came to her in a revelation.

This man on the other side, speaking to them as if they carried the human species' death in their pockets, was in love.

The expression on his face wasn't madness, it was…

Love, she thought. *He loves that woman all the way back on Earth.*

Kane's Whip picked up its pace. Petra knew what that meant. It was reading him, his rage infecting it.

Hector's sabers extended to both sides.

Alistair was gone. He had not just been put back inside the mind that shared the dual personality but thrown, cast away like a stone.

He was so far back, his screams couldn't be heard.

Prometheus had stepped forward the moment he saw the giant, the one who'd taken his wife as a bride. He'd unfurled the Whip without even thinking. He'd only wanted to know two things. The name of the man he was about to kill, and the assurance that it was the right person.

No, the voice said, the only one that could possibly break through Prometheus' grip on the shared mind. While he was in some ways separate from Alistair Kane, he was still a part of him. It was his wife's voice that came through. Luna Kane. *No, Allie. There will be time, but you've learned to move past your recklessness. You learned it back with the Ice Queen. This isn't the paradigm shift you need, and if you cut him down here, all is lost. You'll never come back home to me, and you know it.*

Prometheus gritted his teeth and shoved her back.

He couldn't hold her, though. Where Alistair had failed, Luna did not.

There will be time. You will have your vengeance. Right now, you lead. You kill for yourself later, when it is time. Sheath it, soldier. Sheath the Whip and do as you planned.

Prometheus took a huge breath, and when he exhaled, Alistair was back in control. The hatred was still there, his pulse having finally risen to a normal human's level.

He pressed on his Whip, and it retracted.

Another breath, staring at the man in front of him. His size hadn't mattered. His dual blades. His kill squad behind him. He would have cut this man down, everything else be damned.

Relm is waiting for me, he thought. *Aspen trusted me. A people needs me. There will be time.*

"I come alone. I'm requesting to speak to your Primuses, both on this planet and in your fleet. I'll offer no resistance." He tossed his Whip across the floor. It slid to a stop in front of de Gracilis' foot. "Do you wish to clip me?"

De Gracilis retracted his sabers and hooked them on his back. For the first time, Alistair saw emotion on his face. It was brief and hard to detect, but it was there all the same: disappointment.

He'd wanted this as badly as Alistair.

You'll have it soon enough, Prometheus whispered from somewhere. *I promise you that, big man.*

"No clip," de Gracilis said. "If you change your mind on the way to the Primus, go ahead and ask for your Whip back. You'll die like a warrior."

He squatted easily and picked up the Whip, finding a place on his belt for it. The giant stepped to the side, and the rest of the kill squad formed a path to the train.

Alistair had understood this would happen. All of them were probably under orders to take him alive if possible since the Ascendant would rather make a spectacle of his death than have him fall in these tunnels sight unseen.

Alistair moved through the human tunnel into the train and took a seat at the front.

The rest followed him in.

CHAPTER TWENTY-FOUR

About ten dead lay behind Relm, deep in tunnels that seemed to have no end. The vomit on Obs had been replaced with blood, his maw looking more like a demon's mouth than the lovable drathe's.

Relm couldn't have been happier about the three warriors Aspen had brought along. Those damned gloves were life-savers.

He only had one of the kills.

He looked down at the Commonwealth soldier they'd just killed, the blue substance still eating through the woman's bones. "If we make it out of this, when I get back, one of you three is training me on those. I'm hanging up this pulse."

He meant it.

The three women had moved like hellcats the entire time, working almost as if they were a single person.

"I'll do it," one of them said, "if you train me on the pulse."

"Deal." Relm was having a hard time telling them apart.

The Monaham family all looked like the ice they'd come from—white hair, blue eyes. Practically triplets.

He threw his HUD out in front of his helmet so everyone could see it. They'd been traveling the tunnels for two hours and had no idea where Pro was. The HUD's mapping system was the only thing showing them where they were going, and according to what it now displayed, they were half a kilometer from the place they needed to be.

Obs was staying near Aspen except when he needed to kill. After that, it was right back to the family leader's heels. He was doing a good job. He only knew his single piece, keep Aspen alive, but he was doing it superbly.

"Aspen, to the front," Relm commanded.

De Monaham slid by his warrior.

"Ya done good, kid." Relm felt a little odd calling the leader of an entire world "kid," but that was what he was. He'd still be in the Academy on Earth. "Your time is almost here, and I need you to be ready. Pro didn't bring you down here to kill folks, though your kin here are doing a damned fine job."

He swallowed. There was blood on his cheek. "What's my role?"

"When the fire starts, the four of us here are going to get back to killing and a lot of it. You're going to have tens of thousands of Terram who need to be led. Regardless of what kinda people they are in normal times, they've lost their planet and loved ones. They probably think they've lost everything. They are *not* going to be capable of leading themselves, at least not at first." Relm reached to his belt and pulled off a small comm. "Put this in your ear."

Aspen had turned an even paler shade, but he did as was asked.

"Jeeves is there. Say 'Hello, Jeeves.'"

"Hello, Jeeves," he whispered.

His eyes widened as the AI came through.

"Now, that thing has a camera on it. It's going to show you the layout. Ole Prometheus has already mapped out the way to a weapons cache that hopefully hasn't been raided yet. You get these thousands there, then you do what's in your blood. You send 'em to kill because we're going to need the fire support."

Aspen shook his head. "This makes no sense. Anyone could do this. Any of us. Why in hades would he put me down here?"

The kid was on the verge of collapse.

Relm's hand armor went back, and he slapped him across the face.

"Because fucking Prometheus, bringer of godsdamn fire, said it's your place. That's fucking why. Because your godsdamn liege said it's time to put the mantle of your people on your back and do something."

A red mark bloomed on Aspen's cheek. The three women stepped forward to defend their leader. Obs gave a growl.

Level head, broth, Relm told himself. *Keep it steady.*

"Everybody calm their pants." He looked at the women, then back at Aspen. "I'm not Prometheus, but you think I'm the best fighter he has? Not by a long shot. Yet, he chose me down here. You think he's less protected with his drathe sitting here next to you? No, but that's what he chose. Because he's the best of us, and whether or not any of us sees what he does, *he does*. You were asked here for this specific reason, and I gave you a choice to stay because I knew you weren't a coward. Do I see what he does in ya? Hades, no, but that's not my place to see. *My* part was to get us here, then to get to killin' on the other side of the door we're coming to. Half of my part is done. It's your time now. You got your sister's blood in ya, kid, and I know it ain't yellow. Are you ready to be a warrior?"

He didn't think it was as good a speech as Pro could give, but he'd kept his head, which was what mattered.

The color didn't reappear in Aspen's face, but he nodded. He gritted his teeth, then said, "Let's go."

Relm shook his head and looked down at Obs, his HUD back in his helmet. "You do exactly what Pro told ya." He turned to the three. "I need you banshees to not kill me for slappin' your boss, okay, brothesses? We're all on the same team, and that is Team Get Out of Here A-Fucking-Live, right?"

The near-triplets nodded, stepping back a bit.

Relm sighed. He wasn't built for this shit. He liked his jokes and killing the enemy. This leading stuff was for masochists. "All right. Let's go save the planet."

They fled through the tunnel, finding no one else. They used a few secret passages that appeared to have been vacated a long time ago, but the HUD's blueprint was right, and so was Prometheus. As they moved through the tunnels, he thought he had been more right about the Terram than he'd imagined during his little speech. They hadn't left the jail through these places because they were terrified. They'd watched everything they owned be pillaged and their loved ones die in their arms.

Their only hope was Prometheus, and with so many dead, they wouldn't risk any more.

Relm's helmet cast light down the last tunnel.

"Holy fucking hades," he whispered. A single Terram waited at the end. Short, stout, muscular—a lone man sitting beneath the cavern that waited above.

"*Ave*, Prometheus," Relm called down the tunnel. He turned the audio on his helmet to five and heard the Terram gasp.

He spoke in Relm's language, guttural and rough, but he said, "*Ave, Prometheus.*"

"Thank the gods," Relm whispered and started trotting toward the man. His pulse was at the ready in case this turned into a trick.

"Are you him? Are you Prometheus?" the Terram asked as they arrived.

"No, broth, and I wouldn't wish that burden on anyone, but he sent us. You understand what I'm saying?"

The Terram nodded, and Relm could see him better. His right shoulder was bandaged and his left forearm as well, but he looked functional.

"What are you doing down here?" Relm asked. "You deserting?"

Disgust crossed the Terram's face. "Fuck yourself. I've been waiting for you or Prometheus or someone." He pointed at the circular rock door above him. "Not good up there. The Terram are scared, and there's no leadership. I snuck down here in case anyone came. Small chance, but they say Prometheus is a god, and if anyone else knew these tunnels, he would."

Relm switched his comm to his team. "Aspen, you've

got a group of terrified men, women, and children up there. Some of them are going to be warriors, though. You find whatever Prometheus sees and get them to where they need to go."

"Got it," Aspen came back over the comm. He didn't sound confident, but he didn't sound scared either.

Good enough, Relm thought.

"Are you ready to save us? Is Prometheus?" the Terram asked.

"Hold your corvette, broth. We're here to save folks, but we're waiting for the bossman to give us the signal." He looked at the large rock. "You know how to move it?"

The Terram pounded the rock wall to his left. Relm turned his helmet's light to it. A panel waited there. "It can read your signature?"

The Terram nodded.

"See, broths and brothesses, things are looking up. I thought we were going to have to move the damn thing ourselves." He looked at the Terram. "I'd ask your name, but I know I won't be able to pronounce it, so don't take offense. When I tell you, hit that panel." He looked over his shoulder at the banshees. "I'm going first. You three are right after me, bam, bam, bam like, understand? Anyone short like this little man here, they're on our side. Anyone not short, drop 'em like they're hot."

One of the women smiled at the phrase, but they all nodded.

"Now, my Terram broth, there are more escape tunnels like this, right?"

He nodded.

"Your job, good broth, is to get to the rest of them as

soon as this one clears and open them. My crew here and I will take care of everything above."

"You sure you don't need my help?"

Relm rolled his eyes and thought, *No one wants to do their part. Everyone wants to do something else. Gods bless Pro for dealing with this bullshit.*

"I'm sure," he answered. "Get the rest of the holes open."

The banshee who had smiled whispered, "That's what she said."

Relm whipped around, his face shocked behind his helmet. "Well done."

The Terram didn't get the joke and skipped right over it. "What's next?"

"Next? We wait for bossman to tell us it's time."

"How will we know?" the Terram asked.

Relm rolled his helmet down into his neckline and raised an eyebrow. "This is your first time, I take it? Trust me, when he's ready for us, everyone on this planet is going to know."

Alistair studied the man across the train. They sat facing each other, and Alistair finally let himself take the enemy in.

He didn't have the red eyes of the modified, but Alistair wasn't buying that for a second. The man was a mutant, and whoever had worked on him was the greatest to ever do it. Hector de Gracilis was a marvel. He was the size of Caesar, but there had been no crossbreeding. He was a modified human who dwarfed anything ever done before.

Yet, Alistair felt no fear of the man. Dual-wielding, holding a MechPulse, it didn't matter—the man across the train was dead.

Alistair saw four Martians on the train, wearing the de Gracilis armor. After giving himself some time to think, he'd recognized the de Gracilis name. Only his anger had kept him from seeing clearly in the beginning. The man's grandfather ran Mars and was a propraetor. He'd been the greatest Titan ever to live until Alistair came along. He'd heard the rumors that if Caius had been in his prime, he could have bested Alistair.

Well, after his grandson bled out, they could probably put all those rumors to rest.

The rest of the kill squad was made up of Titans. He didn't recognize any of them, nor did he know any of their callsigns.

A smaller one sat in front of him, her colors a bright blue. Her helmet was retracted, and she had her Whip in her palm.

He could tell she wanted to speak, though orders or propriety was keeping her from doing it.

Alistair leaned back against the train wall. "Got something on your mind, Titan?"

The Titan shot a quick glance at Gracilis to her left. A slight shrug from him, and she turned back. "You were the greatest Titan ever. I heard about you as a child. I saw you march. Why'd you turn to them? You would have gone down as a hero of the Commonwealth for all time. Now you'll die a Subversive. Why?"

Alistair closed his eyes. His mind was still. "What's your call sign, Titan?"

"Aletheia."

Alistair nodded with his eyes still closed. "The god of truth and sincerity. You want the truth, Aletheia, or you want me to give you the line your Ascendant would use?"

She was quiet for a moment. "What would the Imperial Ascendant say?"

Alistair shrugged. "Probably that I was corrupted by power and wealth and wanted to cause destruction for my own purposes. Wanted to burn down the Commonwealth. Sound about right?"

"From where I'm sitting," the Titan said, "that looks exactly like what you want to do."

He gave a small smile. "Do I look wealthy and powerful? But I guess you and he are right. I do want to burn the Commonwealth to the ground, then I want to scatter its ashes to the ends of the universe so they can't be found." He opened his eyes and leaned forward. She gripped her Whip tighter. "You know why? Because it's all a lie. Every single bit, Aletheia, and that's my reason. I decided I couldn't live with those lies anymore."

She held his eyes, not glancing away for a moment.

He leaned back against the train and closed his eyes. The Titan said nothing else.

A half-hour passed in silence.

Alistair's mind wasn't still. He was hardly on the train but pushing himself to new limits. He didn't know if he was like the AllMother with how his mind worked or something new like the mutant sitting across from him, but it didn't matter. He used his gifts, and he moved through the planet as he'd never been able to do while living on it.

As he'd never even tried to.

The train's slowing jolted him, and his eyes flashed open.

It came to a stop, and everyone stood. Kane rose last. They formed another tunnel for him, letting him walk past, with de Gracilis stepping up to walk by his side. It wasn't the mutant's presence that caused the question in his mind, but everything that was to come next.

Luna, he questioned the wife in his mind, *can I do this?*

She didn't pause for a second. *Allie, you better.* He heard the laughter in her voice that he remembered so well as she said, *Do you know how long it's been since I've been laid? Need you to get home and satisfy these needs, my lover.*

Alistair smiled. She might not be here, but his damned mind did a good job of portraying her.

As he was marched through tunnels, he looked straight ahead, letting his mind do the work of his eyes. He was finding it easier now to spread out through the tunnels, caverns, and rooms, his abilities adapting easily to this new command.

De Gracilis was silent next to him, but the mutant's size let Alistair know he was there. It couldn't be denied.

Finally they reached an elevator, and Alistair understood they'd arrived. The time was nearly upon him.

Hector spoke as he touched the panel that opened the doors. "Aletheia and I only up here. You all did well, and I'll make sure your superiors know it." He turned and nodded at them all. Alistair saw that they looked at the mutant with the respect and awe he'd seen in his own followers after the feats he'd accomplished.

They'd follow him to their deaths, he thought.

Soon they'll be able to do just that, Prometheus whispered from behind his door.

The elevator rose again, stopping a half-minute later.

It opened, and Alistair saw the Primus in front of him. He stood at the head of a long rock table, and his leadership team remained standing. Alistair knew the man—Jovan, call sign Hephaestus, god of metallurgy and carpentry but used in the current day for weapons. The man was a master with his Whip, which lay on the table in front of him.

"*Salve,* Hephaestus," Alistair said.

He was present in the room, but also through kilometers and kilometers of this rock world. He was ready.

Hephaestus didn't waste time with pleasantries and didn't bother using the old Odin call sign either. "We know you're not alone, Alistair. Tell us where the rest of your team is, and I promise everyone you brought beneath ground safe passage to Earth. Whatever you wanted to do, you have to know it's impossible. Don't make us kill you."

de Gracilis moved to Alistair's left, facing him. The light blue Titan went to his right. No one was behind him, which was a good thing.

Alistair shrugged. "I'm alone. Here to negotiate terms of surrender."

Hephaestus raised an eyebrow. "Then why go to the other side of the planet? Why not just call it in? I'm not a fool, Alistair."

Alistair was using this time to make sure his mental grip was firm. "If I'd dropped down here, I'd probably be dead. If I did anything up there, I'd risk my fleet before the terms were established. You might think it's stupid, but I'm here alive, as are my people above. It worked."

Hephaestus touched his Whip with his right hand, clearly trusting none of this. "And what terms do you think you can negotiate?"

Prometheus came forward, Alistair giving up control. *See it and die*, he whispered the last of his war mantra. "Complete and total surrender of the Commonwealth. You leave this planet, your fleet disbands, and the Imperial Ascendant steps down from his throne. If you give me that, I'll let some of you live."

Hephaestus smiled. Others at the table laughed or shook their heads.

Prometheus' mind *flexed*.

Quicker than someone could blink, his Whip flew from de Gracilis' belt, landing in his right hand and unfurling.

Air defenses boomed loud enough to shake the room. One after another, missiles, plasma, and lasers shot from the planet's surface, racing through the fiery atmosphere to target the ships just within range.

The sound of laser defense systems could be heard beneath them, cutting down Titan and Martian alike.

Prometheus was on the table and moving before Whips could be activated. He cut down four Titans in mere seconds, finding Hephaestus on the other side and impaling him through his chest.

The room shook as his mind continued to put pressure on the rock around him—the booming sound of weapons outside only increased. The ground beneath his feet rumbled.

He danced off the table as a Whip unfurled to take his

leg off at the knee. He split the attacker's head open as he landed on the floor.

De Gracilis slowly took his sabers out and set them afire.

Pro continued his one-man army, moving through the Titans he'd trained like a boat through calm water, ending their lives with little to no resistance.

He saw de Gracilis grab the light blue Titan's suit, and he pushed her behind him.

There'd been eight Titans in the room. Six were dead. One was on the other side of the table trying to figure out what to do next, and the other was behind the mutant.

"Stand back," de Gracilis said as he stepped forward.

Now it's time, Prometheus thought.

A rock fell to his right, crumbling from the shaking infrastructure. He paid it no mind but kept his mental grip firmly on the weapons outside. Relm would be doing his part now if he still lived.

Pro stepped back onto the table, his Whip at the ready.

The mutant followed him on the other side, sabers at his side.

He'd fought the Ice Queen without using his mind, but he'd never fought like this, split between controlling a planet and physically fighting. Alistair might have thought of such things.

Prometheus didn't. He went forward, bringing fire with him. Not to save…

But to burn.

THE WRITTEN HISTORY OF THE GREAT INSURRECTION

I can't tell you what it was like for Relm, Prometheus, or anyone else.

I can only tell you what I saw from the dreadnought. My leader—my brother—had told me to be ready. That we'd know when to act.

I stood on the bridge next to Faitrin, thinking there'd be no sign. I stood, believing it was over since so much time had passed and we'd heard nothing.

Then the blaze started. I can think of no other way to put it. Across the planet, weapons launched through the fire, heading for the fleet that held sway over everything.

Pro had seen the truth, even if no one else had. The Commonwealth had moved just beyond the fiery atmosphere, within a half kilometer or so. I later learned *why* they'd done it: they had been trying to cut down the time required to deliver their soldiers to the war against the Terram. The underground men and women had fought so fiercely that the Commonwealth wanted every second they could get.

After the planet was claimed, they'd remained.

Why not? No one would be firing.

Until Prometheus had shown up.

The barrage spread across the planet, hitting ships of all sizes. They started to fall into the fiery atmosphere almost immediately.

We knew what to do.

The war for Phoenix had begun.

A thousand years after a young woman had left Earth, the first true challenge to the empire had arrived.

The story continues with *Titan's Return,* available at Amazon and through Kindle Unlimited.

Claim your copy today!

When Michael and I were outlining this series, we wrote it in three arcs. The first arc was Alistair becoming a warlord, the second was him building his army, and the final arc was him returning home.

If you've made it this far, you've reached the end of the second arc, and for that, I am thankful (as is Michael).

As a writer, I truly enjoyed creating the first two arcs, but in comparison to the final three books? Well...to put it in kid-lingo, the first two were like Easter, and the final was Christmas.

The first six books in this series really let you dig in and get to know the characters on a personal level. You understand them as if they live in the same house with you, and that's all necessary for a story to have a fantastic payoff.

The last three books? Get ready for an action-filled roller coaster, in which you're watching the people you love, hate, and those you love to hate, all try to fulfill the desires you've come to know so well.

I'm was excited to write the last arc, and I might be even more excited you're about to read it.

Also, and this is important: someone told Mike about this being a love story. It might've been Steve – who knows… Whatever you do, do not tell him about the ending to book six. He'll kill me.

Book 7 is right around the corner. *Ave*, reader.

All the best,
db

Thank you for not only reading this book but this entire series so far and these author notes as well.

So, I don't have David's author notes yet, so I can't respond to them.

He's LATE! Or I'm early writing my author notes. *But I doubt that.*

LMBPN - an Entertainment company.

Believe it or not, I had envisioned LMBPN (my publishing company) as an entertainment company back in 2015. Much like IBM (which was a typewriter company when it started, but IBM stands for International Business Machines), I figured LMBPN is more than just a book publishing company.

Mind you, when I was dreaming big LMBPN had one (1) author, me, and three books.

I'd like to say we came from very (*very*) humble beginnings. On my third day as a published author, I think I made something like $0.97 cents.

Over the years, we've published many collaborations with some great authors, and some of our fans have started working with us to help in several areas.

Right now – just under six years from when I published Death Becomes Her – the company has over 1,200 books released in English. About 700-800 of those are released in paperback. We have over 100 books translated, most in German. We're also translating into French, Italian, Spanish, and Dutch.

LMBPN has produced over 200+ Audiobooks and licensed out over 400 more to other companies.

We are looking into comics, children's books, and Romance. (Don't tell Zen-Master Steve™ or Editor-Supreme-Lynne™, or I might have uncomfortable questions thrown my way. I'm in Cabo, so I'll plead sunstroke if you do.)

We are reviewing AI efforts with Google, looking into using the Unreal Engine for Machinima efforts and AI voices, and eventually will have our Kurtherian Gambit soundtrack for sale.

All while releasing over 300 titles in 2021.

We have other projects moving along, but those are under wraps for now.

On the downside, we have no projects going with James Patterson... *Dammit!*

Well, that's it for now for me. David should discuss with you the new trilogy he has in the works... But if he doesn't...

Well, ask him on Facebook ;-)

May you have a great week or weekend, wherever you are!

Ad Aeternitatem,
Michael Anderle

Nemesis

She's coming and no one can stop her...

An alien Queen, Morena, was removed from power and forced into exile. Doomed to roam space forever, with no hope of return.

Until a random party brings a man named Michael to her crashed ship. For the first time in millennia, Morena sees her salvation. First, in Michael ... and then Earth. The perfect place to repopulate her species. And those already here? **They can bow or die.**

As Morena begins her conquest, can Michael warn the world before it's too late? Can anyone stop the most powerful force the world has ever seen?

Earth's final Nemesis has arrived.

Don't miss this pulse-pounding science fiction series! If you love thought provoking thrill-rides, grab this book today!

The Singularity

One thousand years in the future, humans no longer rule...

In the early twenty-first century, humanity marveled at its greatest creation: Artificial Intelligence. They never foresaw the consequences of such a creation, though...

Now, in a world where humans must meet specifications to continue living, a man named Caesar emerges. Different, both in thought and talent, Caesar somehow slipped through the genetic net meant to catch those like him.

Eyes are falling on Caesar now, though, and he can no longer hide. The Artificial Intelligence wants him dead, but others want him to lead their revolution...

Can one man stand against humanity's greatest creation? A don't-miss epic science fiction novel that pits one man fighting for the future of all people!

Red Rain

What would you do if you couldn't stop killing?

John Hilt lives The American Dream. His corner office looks out on Dallas's beautiful skyline. His amazing wife and children love him. His father and sister adore him. John has it all.

Except every few years, when Harry shows back up. Harry wants John to kill people. Harry wants to watch the world burn.

Murderous thoughts take hold of John, and as flames ignite across his life, the sky doesn't send cool rain water, but blood to feed their hunger.

If you love taut, psychological thrillers, grab Red Rain today and prepare to sleep with the lights on!

The Devil's Dream

He'll raise the dead, at all costs...

Perhaps the smartest man to ever live, Matthew Brand changed the world by twenty-five years old. In his mid-thirties, he still shaped the world as he wanted, until cops gunned down his son on the street.

Brand's life changed then. He forgot about bettering Earth and started trying to resurrect his son.

Eventually, Brand's mind overpowered even death's mysteries; he discovered how to bring back the dead--he only needed living bodies to make his son's life possible again. Why not use the bodies of those who killed his son? In the largest manhunt the FBI's ever experienced, how do they stop a man who can calculate all the odds and stack them in his favor?

CONNECT WITH THE AUTHORS

Connect with David and sign up for his email list here:

Email list
http://www.davidbeersauthor.com/mailing-list

Website
http://www.davidbeersfiction.com/

Social Media:

https://www.facebook.com/davidbeersauthor

Email List: http://lmbpn.com/email/

Connect with Michael and sign up for his email list here:

Website: http://lmbpn.com

Email List: http://lmbpn.com/email/

Social Media:

https://www.facebook.com/LMBPNPublishing

https://twitter.com/MichaelAnderle

https://www.instagram.com/lmbpn_publishing/

https://www.bookbub.com/authors/michael-anderle